Ann J. Johnson Paxson, Edward M. Paxson

Memoirs of the Johnson family

With an Autobiography

Ann J. Johnson Paxson, Edward M. Paxson

Memoirs of the Johnson family
With an Autobiography

ISBN/EAN: 9783337031244

Printed in Europe, USA, Canada, Australia, Japan

Cover: Foto ©Raphael Reischuk / pixelio.de

More available books at **www.hansebooks.com**

MEMOIRS

OF THE

JOHNSON FAMILY:

WITH AN

AUTOBIOGRAPHY.

BY
ANN J. PAXSON.

PRINTED BY
J. B. LIPPINCOTT COMPANY.
1885.

INTRODUCTORY.

It is not my purpose to add to this little volume. A few words of explanation, however, may be proper. Many years ago my dear mother, at the request of my wife and myself, commenced to note down some of the incidents of her life, which included many reminiscences of our family history. We were the more desirous she should do so from the fact that otherwise the large store of such information which she possessed would be lost in a great measure to her descendants. Her sister, Elizabeth Pickering, was then deceased; her brother, William H. Johnson, died a few years thereafter, and she was left the only survivor of the family.

The work thus commenced became a labor of

love and grew upon her hands. This volume far exceeds in size anything she originally contemplated, and was left in my care to revise, alter, or amend, as in my opinion might be thought judicious. Its publication was also left to my judgment, with the understanding, however, that if published at all, it was to be privately printed for the gratification of those who had known and loved her while living, and who cherished her memory after her death.

The book is printed precisely as she wrote it, one or two passages only having been omitted, containing personal allusions, and the omission of which had been suggested by herself.

It is now printed, not only for the preservation of the incidents contained therein, but from a sense of filial regard for each of my parents, whose memory I shall ever cherish with the warmest feelings of affection and gratitude. Of the two, my dear father occupies the less conspicuous position in this volume; but this arises solely from the fact that it was intended principally as a memoir of the Johnson family. I cannot, however, allow the occasion to pass without an expression of my appreciation of his

many excellencies of character. A son is seldom fitted to be the biographer of a parent, and
I shall not attempt such a duty; but I feel constrained here to say that he was a man of varied
information, and possessed a vigorous, clear
mind and sound judgment. It was these latter
traits which gave him the weight and influence
he enjoyed in the community in which he lived,
and especially in the religious society of which
he was for so many years a conspicuous and
useful member. Whatever he had to do he
did well.

The married life of my parents was singularly
felicitous. Its harmony was never interrupted.
They were married October 22, 1817. An impromptu gathering of their friends occurred on
October 22, 1867, which was the fiftieth anniversary of their marriage. The pleasant memories
of this occasion yet linger in the recollections of
many who were present. A further reference
to the pleasure it afforded our parents will be
found in this volume. They survived their
golden wedding many years, in the enjoyment
of good health and a bright and cheerful old
age. My father died on the nineteenth of

Fourth month, 1881, in the eighty-eighth year
of his age, and my mother on the twenty-first
of Third month, 1883, in her ninety-second
year. They were buried in the yard belonging
to Buckingham Friends' Meeting, where rest
my ancestors for three generations. They died
as they had lived, consistent members of that
excellent society, the Society of Friends. The
Master's summons found them with their loins
girt, their staff in their hands, and their lamp
burning.

The memory of good parents should always
be cherished. The influence of good lives cannot be too long perpetuated. It strengthens
those who, following in their footsteps, strive
to emulate their virtues.

My heart swells as I recall the home of my
childhood, illuminated by their blessed presence, precept, and example. The quiet farm-
house, with its holy memories, is within sight
as I write these lines. The happy hours of
boyhood come up before me like a flood.
And while new duties and responsibilities have
arisen with advancing years, and a reasonable
amount of success has rewarded my labors, I

attribute it in large measure to the example of
fidelity to duty and the high standard of Christian excellence which was always so prominently
before me in my happy childhood's home.

E. M. P.

Bycot House, 1885.

MEMOIRS.

I WILL commence this account of our relatives with a glimpse of my grandfather, William Johnson. This is, unfortunately, all I am able to give; the little I have gleaned from his history was obtained from his widow when I was a mere child. He was taken from his family so early in life that his children were too young to appreciate any part of his character but his fondness for themselves.

He was a native of Ireland,* which country

---

* While William Johnson undoubtedly came to this country from Ireland, later information leads me to believe that he was of English descent. The branch of the family to which William belonged settled in Ireland. I regret that we have not more information concerning this learned and accomplished man. I have in my possession a few volumes of the library which he brought to this country, also a mahogany desk in good preservation. Another of his descendants, Dr. Thomas Johnson, of Readington, New Jersey, has four manuscript lectures on scientific subjects, written in the beautiful, round hand

2   9

he left for the new world in early manhood; his motives for the change may perhaps be explained by the motto on the family coat of arms: "UBI LIBERTAS, IBI PATRIA." He may have seen, even then, the cloud that overshadowed his beloved native land, and possibly discerned in prophetic vision her subsequent fearful struggle with oppression and power.

---

of William Johnson,—so beautiful as to be mistaken for copper-plate printing. They are dated in 1763. I remember reading, when a boy, one of his manuscript lectures on electricity, to which science he appears to have paid particular attention. He had one of the best, if not the best, loadstones in this country, which he used to illustrate his lectures on magnetism. It was afterwards presented to Princeton College, under the following circumstances. Calling one day at the college upon a visit to its president, he found that gentleman and his wife amusing themselves by picking up needles with a small loadstone. Professor Johnson at once sent over to his own house for his large stone, and astonished the president and his wife by picking up with it a large pair of fire-tongs with the shovel tied to them. He then presented the stone to the college, and it is now among the curiosities of the college museum. He also presented to the same college the original electrical machine made by Benjamin Franklin.—E. M. P.

He was the only one of the brothers that chose America as an abiding place, though Jervis Johnson, a minister in the Society of Friends, travelled through it in that capacity, and visited his brother's grave in Charleston, South Carolina. I have only a faint recollection of him, but Timothy Paxson, of Philadelphia, told me he had never, in the course of his life, met with so much innocence and simplicity of manners and character, united with so much intelligence.

His son, who bore his name, had preceded him a year in his visit among us, and expected to return with him, had he lived to do so, but while bathing in the Schuylkill with some of his young associates he was drowned,—cramp the supposed cause, for he was an expert swimmer. He was buried two days before his father arrived in Philadelphia.

He bore the sad tidings of the death of his youngest and darling son with true Christian fortitude, walked the room a few minutes in silence, then sat down and calmly inquired the particulars.

I have reason to believe that William and Jervis were all the brothers that remained in religious communion with the religious society in which they were educated.

Their sister was married to a nobleman, and it is not improbable that this connection, as it would draw her from her early associates, might have influenced others of the family. Tradition has not mentioned whether she inherited the various talents of her kindred, but we know, from reliable sources, that she was considered one of the handsomest women in Ireland, and it appears her titled husband was satisfied with the amount of her qualifications. But to return from this digression.

My grandfather, when he crossed the ocean, brought with him four hundred volumes of the standard works of the time, and most of them would seem calculated for all time, as they hold their position steadfastly in the estimation of the public. They were divided after his death among his children. Of those that came to my father's share were Hume's History of England, many volumes of the British Classics, Homer's Iliad and Odyssey, Young's Night Thoughts, Milton's Paradise Lost, Virgil, and Goldsmith. The delight these afforded me, even in childhood, can only be imagined and measured by those who have at so early a period of life tasted a similar enjoyment, and the tenacity of early memory has left on my mind the impression of their flights of poetic fancy and their still more useful and valuable truths.

At the time of his death he was only thirty-five years of age, and was engaged in delivering lectures on scientific subjects; those on electricity I well remember seeing in my father's house. They were characterized by beauty of language and elegance of penmanship.

My father, about the meridian of life, met with a lady in Trenton who had known his parents in their early wedded days. She described William Johnson as a model of manly beauty, with the most winning urbanity of manners and a liberality of spirit that she never saw surpassed, though his munificence was more in accordance with his natural temperament than with his means of indulging it.

The portrait Curran draws of a genuine Irish gentleman coincides so completely with the accounts we have received of his character that I am induced to transcribe a portion of it:

"The hospitality of other countries is a matter of necessity or convention: in savage nations of the first, in polished, of the latter. But the hospitality of an Irishman is not the running account of posted and ledgered courtesies, as in other countries; it springs, like all his qualities, his faults, his virtues, directly from the heart. The heart of an Irishman is by nature bold, and he confides; it is tender, and he loves; it is generous, and he gives; it is social, and he is hospitable."

Such was my grandfather, and I have a pleasure and pride in believing that he has descendants who do not discredit their noble ancestry.

William Johnson, after about two years' residence in America, married Ruth Potts, of Trenton, New Jersey. Her brother, with whom she lived, was then mayor of that city, and a very influential man. I know not how many years succeeding their marriage they remained there, but my father, who was their third child, was born in Philadelphia.

After her husband's death, in Charleston, South Carolina, his widow and children came back to Trenton and witnessed the battle at that place. When standing in her own door, after the conflict was over, an aged man said to her in passing by, "Mrs. Johnson, if war is right there is nothing wrong."

He was giving directions to some boys, one of them her son, then fourteen years old, who were removing the dead bodies on sleds to the place of interment.

Grandmother soon after gave Philadelphia the preference as a home, having many friends in that city. While a resident there she became acquainted with Oliver Paxson, a man of very high position, not only in the Society of Friends, of which he was a prominent member, but in the community at large. Their union was the result, and he brought her and her youngest daughter, Ruth, to his beautiful home on the banks of the Delaware, near Coryell's Ferry, now the village of New Hope. A happy home, made still happier by the best of step-mothers, as his two daughters by a former marriage always termed her. They lived thirty years together in happiness as entire as perhaps ever falls to the lot of mortals. She survived him a few years, and closed her earthly career at the home of her youngest child, who had married her husband's nephew, Timothy Paxson, of Philadelphia.

Of her kindred I have personally known but little; one of her nieces, Rebecca Potts, became the wife of George Sherman, for many years editor of the *Trenton Federalist*. Another niece, Rebecca Horner, married with George M. Coates, of Philadelphia. Her nephew, Joseph P. Horner, was well known in his native city, for amiability and poetic talent; he married Jane West, who survived him several years, and was considered an ornament to the circle in which she moved. Joseph P. Horner was for several years afflicted with loss of sight; I will subjoin the poem he wrote after a successful operation for cataract:

Father, allow the tears to flow
   Of joy, of gratitude to Thee ;
That this most glorious truth I know,
   That I was blind, but now I see.

As when the fiat from Thy lips,
   Called from the depths of darkness, light ;
Thy will, the terrible eclipse
   Has banished from my shadowed sight.

I see once more the teeming earth,
   In all its garniture of pride ;
And living waters gushing forth
   From many a green hill's sunny side.

The rich reward the harvest gave,
  I see on every fertile plain;
And my own river's gentle wave,
  Still gliding onward to the main.

I see the beams of rising day,
  Through golden mists of morning glance;
And in the noontide's fervid ray,
  The rippling brook's bright waters dance.

And, oh! far sweeter as they rise
  Group over group, it is to see
In many a dear one's kindling eyes
  The answering glance of sympathy.

Oh! when by power Divine unsealed
  To vision burst these orbs of sight,
How every object stood revealed,
  In robes of beauty and of light!

The varied scenes around me brought,
  The fair, the beautiful, the grand,—
All form one wondrous picture wrought
  By Thine, the mighty Master's Hand.

SARAH, the eldest child of William and Ruth Johnson, became the wife of Thomas Matthews, of Virginia; he was engaged in mercantile business in Alexandria, and, during his visits to Philadelphia to purchase goods, became acquainted with his future wife. She went to his home immediately after their marriage. Several years subsequently they removed to her native city with their four boys, two of them in their minority.

It is difficult to speak of the subject of this memoir without a fear of incurring the charge of exaggeration from partiality; her talents and accomplishments were appreciated in a degree at least by her cotemporaries, but the virtues that illumed her rare character could only be known by the comparatively few that mingled with her in close social communion. More than half a century ago, in a large company in the city, I heard the following lines applied to her by a gentleman of the circle. A lady responded, "I know of no person but Sarah Matthews to whom they are entirely applicable."

> Thy gentle mission all fulfilled,
>   Thy courage by no ills dismayed;
> Thy patience by no wrongs subdued,
>   Thy gay good humor, can they fade?

I leave this part of a subject to which I feel my inability to do justice, and turn to other matters connected with her daily life.

Perhaps the power of her creative pencil contributed more to her happiness than any other circumstance, for her fondness for painting was completely a passion, and it required all her force of character to keep it in subjection, and prevent its interference with the daily routine of life's duties. She was self-taught, but surpassed most of those who had spent much time in the study of that attractive art; several of her pictures were exhibited in the Academy of Fine Arts, and elicited much notice and admiration. A landscape attracted most attention, worked with a needle on white satin; it was universally pronounced a splendid specimen of embroidery.

A friend of mine walking through the Academy saw some Englishmen of her acquaintance examining the landscape with special interest, and one of them observed, "What a fine price that picture would command in our country." A decided compliment, when we consider that these gentlemen were amateurs on this subject, and were then making the tour of America to view the curiosities of nature and art.

She possessed considerable poetical talent, but never much cultivated it; it was lost in her absorbing fondness for its sister art. Her death, which occurred in Philadelphia at the age of fifty years, seemed premature to the many who had known and loved her; but, as "that life is long which answers life's great end," she probably accomplished more than most whose earthly life has been of longer date, and the messenger that brought her release from its cares and trials was evidently a welcome guest.

Of her four sons, two died early and unmarried; the remaining two had many of her talents, among them poetry and painting. Thomas, the eldest, was many years professor of mathematics in the College of Kentucky; he married

his cousin Harriet, eldest daughter of Thomas
P. Johnson, and one of the most beautiful women
of her day. A celebrated American artist, who
had visited all the courts of Europe, assured one
of her family that he had never met with a face
and form so perfect.

A cotemporary poetess alluded to that circumstance in the following lines :

They who in many a foreign clime,
  Had owned of beauty's charms the power ;
Where rose the feudal hall sublime,
  Or bloomed the rose-wreathed myrtle bower ;

Admiring scanned with curious glance
  The rich saloon, the courtly hall,
The social group, or festive dance,—
  Confessed *thee* loveliest of all.

But that matchless eloquence of eye and manner, that seemed to possess an irresistible charm,
are now perhaps faintly remembered by her few
surviving cotemporaries.

"Such are your triumphs, Death and Time."

Caleb Bently Matthews, her youngest son,
was a physician ; he graduated in the allopathic
school of medicine, and practised in Philadel-

phia. He, however, eventually became a convert to the homœopathic system, and was a professor in that college at the time of his death.

While a student he wrote secretly some lines of poetry on the walls of the university, and had much amusement in hearing his fellow-students dispute about their authorship; they were attributed by some to Moore, and by others to Byron.

The verses doubtless took a coloring from the state of his own mind; his beloved mother was no more, and his father, who never understood his temperament, was anxious to make a mechanic of him; this his repugnance prevented, and he commenced the study of medicine under rather inauspicious circumstances. But his talent and energy conquered all difficulties; he became eminent in his profession, and, though he did not attain old age, left to his widow and children an ample competence.

TO ——. WRITTEN ON THE WALLS OF THE UNIVERSITY.

Vainly thou bidst me wake again,
  Some feeling of my earlier hours;
I cannot tune the magic strain,
  That strewed my youthful path with flowers.

Oh! then I wandered fancy free,
Through fairy realms of poesy.

Fleeting are joy's delusive forms,
   And all that they have left to me
Is cheerless, as the bitter storms
   That howl through blasted forest tree.
      For hope, to me, is like the ray
      That half illumes a winter day.

Yet, there are still some gleams of bliss,
   That on my darkened spirit break,
Pure as the hallowed rays that kiss
   The bosom of the tranquil lake;
      When Luna's silver orb on high
      Sheds lustre through a cloudless sky.

And as Aurora, dawning bright,
   Brings nature's darkened scenes to view,
So memory's benignant light
   Joy's faded visions can renew;
      And bring them forth in bright array,
      As when they dawned in youth's fair day.

Like burnished clouds, when day is o'er,
   That gather round the sun's decline;
Some joys, when rapture is no more,
   Still linger 'round this heart of mine.
      And o'er my soul their milder ray
      Will shed, till feeling fades away.

In the previous sketches I have drawn I felt no hesitation in saying all that came before my mind. It is true, that of the first my materials were very limited; but I used them all, well knowing no other had ever appropriated them.

In the second instance I distrusted my ability to render to a character so uncommon her full due, but felt no apprehension of a "tale twice told."

The case of Thomas P. Johnson stands, however, on different ground. So much has been written, both of his public and private life, that little remains to be told.

The pictorial history of New Jersey, his adopted State, has a long and highly interesting article, defining his position in that place. His history, therefore, as a lawyer and as a man, is already before the public; but as this memoir is exclusively for the family circle, it may be admissible to introduce some anecdotes of his early

24

days that might not interest the community at large.

One circumstance I do not recollect to have seen mentioned which deserves notice, not only as a beautiful tribute to his merit, but manifests the appreciation of his legal friends, that, after a lapse of twenty years, he should retain so evidently his place in their regard. Many years after he had relinquished the practice of law and had gone to reside with his daughter, wife of the late Dr. R. D. Corson, of New Hope, the members of the Flemington bar sent a skilful artist to paint a portrait of him, to be suspended over the judge's seat in Flemington court-house, where it remains at present, a most life-like picture.

Some years after it was placed there, his nephew, Edward Paxson, of Philadelphia, gave a temperance lecture in that house in the evening. Seeing, by the imperfect light, features that were familiar, he approached with a lamp and uttered an exclamation of surprise and pleasure. Lawyer Clark then inquired, "Did you know him?" When informed of the relationship he responded, "Why did you not tell

4

us that sooner? Had it been known that a
nephew of Mr. Johnson was to lecture, we
should have had all Jersey to hear you."

His power as an advocate has, I presume,
never been questioned; but I remember one
evidence of it that I will narrate here. When
a young girl, while on a visit to my aunt in the
city, some of her family went to New Jersey to
hear a trial that had claimed a large share of
public attention.

A daughter of Judge Stockton had been slan-
dered, and her father applied to uncle to defend
her, saying, "I do not call upon you as a lawyer,
but as a friend and relative." He was uncle to
the advocate's wife. I was still at my aunt's
when the party returned, and Benjamin Paxson
was the reporter. He said, "I heard that rich
and full-toned voice before I got near the court-
house. The audience seemed transfixed by his
eloquence, and I never heard it equalled." Ten
thousand pounds damages were awarded to
plaintiff.

There was a period in his youthful days when
" bout-rhymes" were a very fashionable amusement in mixed company, and must have af-

forded much entertainment. The terminating word only of each line was given, the rest of the line supplied by those to whom the task was assigned. On one of these occasions a pretty and witty young lady gave to the subject of this notice the words *please, tease, bemoan,* and *bone.* He almost immediately handed her the following:

To a form that is faultless, a face that must—please,
Is united a restless desire to—tease;
Oh! how my hard fate I should always—bemoan,
Did I think she would ever be, bone of my—bone.

Instances of his readiness in repartee might be given to an almost indefinite extent, showing that he had that attribute of his remote relative, Dr. Johnson, not inaptly termed the "Giant of English Literature." My uncle could, I believe, trace the kindred tie, without a link wanting in the chain of evidence.

At one time, being at a public watering-place where a book was kept for visitors to register their names, two of the guests wrote each three pages. Thomas P. Johnson next took the pen,—

Here's Parker and Bringhurst, two imps of the muse,
  By a fondness for scribbling inspired,
Six pages have written, as dull as old news;
  I have read it, and now I am tired.

I will now close this imperfect sketch of my gifted uncle. He died at New Hope, in the seventy-seventh year of his age. The New Jersey Supreme Court passed a series of resolutions expressive of respect, admiration, and regret, and the members of the Flemington bar attended almost in a body to witness the remains of him whose brilliant career they had long been familiar with, consigned to its kindred clay.

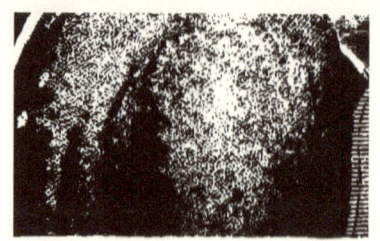

SAMUEL JOHNSON.

THE pen that noticed William Johnson and two of his descendants must not be silent as regards the third, my affectionate and beloved father.

Soon after his death I wrote a biographical sketch that was published, giving a pretty full account both of his pursuits and character; and, though countless recollections continually arise relative to him, I know not that I can add much to what has been written that will interest those less immediately connected with him.

I will, however, give an extract from a letter I received soon after his death; the allusion to him is as beautiful as appropriate:

I have often thought of thee since the death of thy sainted father; so purified from the dross of this earth before he had left it. Although you must feel his loss greatly, you must also feel that you have everything to console you in his life and in his death.

Like the sun, he has run his full course; wherever

he has shone, there has been warmth and life, beauty and gladness. The intellectual garden has blossomed, the bird-like melodies of affectionate hearts have risen on the air, and his work at length accomplished, he has sunk calmly to his rest, leaving even the clouds that must hang over your horizon tinged with his departing glory.

He had from very early life a fondness for poetic composition, and occasionally indulged in it, but in the meridian of manhood the management of his large farm, with much public business, left him little time for his favorite pursuit. The largest portion of his poems were written in what may be termed the decline of life. I will append to this memento of him an article written in a young lady's album, after he had considerably exceeded threescore and ten years:

> Lady, I thus meet thy request;
> Else should I not have deemed it best
> To scribble on this spotless page
> With the weak trembling pen of age.
> I've written in Time's album long;
> Sketches of life, with moral song;
> Blotted in haste full many a leaf
> Whose list of beauties might be brief;
> Should I some pleasing views now glean,
> 'Twould make at best a winter scene;

On the bleak side of seventy years,
How sear the foliage appears.
And frost-nipt flowers we strive in vain
By culture to revive again.
The snows of Time my temples strew,
Warning to bid the Muse adieu.

I had intended here to close this memoir, but an impromptu of an earlier date having arisen in my mind, I concluded to insert it. To me the incident that induced it is full of pleasant memories, and afforded amusement to a large circle of young people. It was to him the work of a few minutes.

In the year 1815 there was a social gathering at my father's house. It was a lovely summer day, and among the guests present were Sidney Coates, Julianna Randolph, and Elizabeth Snowden, of Philadelphia, three of my early friends, who attended my marriage in 1817. The incident referred to was impressed upon my memory by a visit they paid me at Woodlawn in 1866, when it was discussed between us, with other pleasant memories of the past.

The occasion I allude to was a bridal party. Among the guests was a medical graduate, who

seemed largely to participate in the hilarity of
the day, and by his sprightliness added to the
gayety that conspicuously prevailed. He requested four of the girls to present him a heart,
assuring them he would be entirely satisfied
with such as any one of them could bestow, if
inclined to do so.

It did not seem remarkable at all to me that
such an idea should have taken possession of his
fancy, for of the stranger maidens one had radiant eyes, and was of queenly bearing; another,
from the same locality, "Serene as the moonlight, and warm as the day."

The girls applied to retired to another apart-
ment to compare views before making this important surrender, and were united in judgment
that a paper heart would be the most fitting material for the occasion, and the only one they had
then and there to dispose of. One was soon prepared, and with the aid of pen and ink divided
into sections, most of the unamiable traits to
which human nature is liable had there

"A local habitation and a name."

In the smallest section of all was written the

word love. When we handed it to our friend he professed to feel great disappointment that its texture was so unlike the one he hoped to attain; yet even this he prized highly, and should keep it forever,—alas!

> "That term does not to time belong,
> It has no meaning like forever."

After its merits had been discussed, the recipient put it in his pocket-book, and the conversation took a different turn. A proposal was made to visit the Natural Well in a meadow on the farm, and not far distant, called by the Indians Holicong. History and tradition had united to invest this place with deep interest, for there William Penn held a treaty with the red men of the forest, and we were accustomed to consider it classic ground.

The witcheries of romance and poetry, too, had been brought into requisition, and the bard had sung,—

> "That round Holicong fountain
> The maize and the deer would the Hunter Chief bring."

It had also been the origin of some attractive and fanciful tales from the pen of a youthful

5

writer in that vicinity. But I must not dwell
over-long on these dear familiar scenes, much as
memory delights there to linger, but pursue my
onward narrative, mindful of the traveller, who,
when the shades of evening are about to over-
take him, may not stoop to gather the daisies in
his pathway, nor "snatch a blossom from the
bough."

On our return from Holicong, the bride and
groom picked up a paper that father had caused
to be thrown there in our absence. "What is
this," exclaimed the latter,—"some spiritual
agency?" We all collected round him while
he read the following lines:

Good Heavens! A heart, but such a one
As none need wish to call his own;
Made up of follies, whim, and glee,
Without one grain of charity.
Without one virtue to decoy,
Without one avenue to joy,
So void of good, so poor a heart,
That love made up its smallest part.
Oh! give a heart such each could give,
With which I should be proud to live,
A life's devotion I would prove,
But, oh! a little more of love.

After a due portion of comment, the verses were laid by with the heart, and this happy day, like all others, had its dawn and close; but it will live in memory.

RUTH PAXSON.

THIS, the fourth and youngest of my grand-father's children, became the wife of Timothy Paxson, of Philadelphia, whither she removed immediately after her marriage. Her youthful days had glided serenely by at the home of her mother and step-father on the banks of the Delaware.

In this quiet, rural retreat her mind was pre-pared, by reading and reflection, to become a shining light to a large circle of admiring and gifted friends in her city home. Her husband, too, being a man of strong intellectual powers and varied acquirements, their residence soon became the resort of persons of distinguished taste and literature. Many of the prominent writers of her day were accustomed to subject their works to her criticism. Among these was Joseph Sansom, author of "American Letters from Europe," and Charles B. Brown, the novelist. She was a correct and elegant writer, and had an extensive correspondence with some of the most celebrated literati of that period. In a few instances it took exclusively the poetical form, and of this number was that of William Wilkins, a young lawyer of much talent and great promise, cut off by consumption in the bloom of life.

I often, in girlhood, read their correspondence, and will copy here some lines of it that still linger in my memory. This I do the more willingly, as I have reason to believe that no copy of it now exists, as all her letters and manuscripts were burned in her son Edward's house, which was destroyed by fire some years after her death. He expressed more regret for this loss than anything else it contained. In comparison, the destruction of his law-library was a small item in his view.

EXTRACT FROM A LETTER TO STELLA.

Shall the weak youth, around whose hapless brow
   No lambent light of genius ever played,
See awed opponents to his judgment bow,
   And hoary judges by his wisdom swayed?

For him shall fame a laureate wreath prepare,
   And praise in grateful incense breathe around;
Shall Stella watch him with maternal care,
   And bid her living lyre his name resound.

Fair but delusive hope my fate denies,
   Each flattering view thy beamy pencil draws;
I gaze, the quick tears rush into my eyes
   And dim the dazzling plumes of proud applause.

But soon relentless death must mar the scene,
   Nor Clara's smiles, nor Stella's strains can save;
Yet will your gentle cares from anguish screen
   And smooth the thorny passage to the grave.

The above fragment of their correspondence, thus rescued from entire oblivion, was written three weeks previous to his death. Stella, the subject of this memoir, was by him regarded with feelings of grateful friendship; Clara, with those of the most devoted love. She was subsequently the wife of President Madison.

In the years 1805 and 1806, a literary paper, called the *Evening Fire-Side*, was published in Philadelphia, established and principally supported by the Society of Friends.

Ruth Paxson and her cousin, Joseph P. Horner,

were among the most conspicuous of the contributors. Her pieces were mostly over the signatures "Roland," "Matilda," and "Sophia." A prose essay, with the last mentioned, I will copy at the close of this memoir, because it affords a better specimen of her style, and gives more idea of the writer's character than any I could probably select. Her contributions were mostly in poetry. One of these I will transcribe, as that paper is by the readers of the present day almost forgotten, having been superseded by such a countless number of periodicals, but it had its day of interest as well as usefulness.

COMPOSED ON THE BANKS OF THE DELAWARE, DURING THE PREVALENCE OF THE YELLOW FEVER, IN 1802.

Gentle stream, whose tiny billows
Now thy flowery borders lave;
Now display the bending willows
Pictured in the dimpling wave.

On thy verdant margin straying,
Torn from many a tender tie;
Thy meandering course surveying,
Hear a wretched wanderer sigh.

Soon, with nature's treasures laden,
   Thou shalt reach the crowded shore,
.Where yon city's rising splendors
   Echo to the dashing oar.

There immersed in toil and danger,
   While the anxious moments roll,
To domestic joys a stranger,
   Sighs the partner of my soul.

Death his pensive step pursuing,
   Pestilence around him glares;
Wakeful love his pillow strewing
   With a thousand tender cares.

Languid limbs and heaving bosom,
   Fell disease's dreadful train;
From each soft domestic duty
   My reluctant steps detain.

Source of Being, God of Mercy,
   Hear a suppliant's earnest prayer;
Spare the husband, friend, and brother,
   Every fond connection spare.

But if my presumptuous wishes
   Dare to cross Thy wise design,
Teach my tortured soul submission,
   Bend my stubborn will to Thine.

Or in more transcendent mercy,
　　From the load of mortal woes,
In Thy all Paternal bosom
　　Bid my wearied soul repose.

In introducing the essay spoken of on a previous page, I am reminded of an incident connected with it that adds to its interest, in my view, and may possibly with those that shall in future read this record of olden time. An old gentleman of our neighborhood, a retired physician, often visited at our house. He had considerable influence in his day, though rather vain and pedantic; but what was not comprehended sometimes passed for wisdom,—perhaps not the only instance in the world that this mistake has been made. An old lady told me that he was the most sensible man she had ever conversed with, for she never understood him; rather a severe criticism, but not meant as such, for she was really surprised

"That one small head could carry all he knew."

It was, however, a striking comment on the obscurity that involved his conversation.

He was very old-school on many points, even

for that period, particularly on the subject of female rights. As he was quite a reader, he took considerable interest in mother's society, notwithstanding their opinions on this favorite topic were entirely at variance. But he was anxious to make a convert of her, and often brought to aid him in the task works calculated to impress on female minds (that had not counteracting influences) the belief that household duties alone should engross their attention, while the mind, the "God-given" mind, might remain an empty waste, as regards mental culture, without loss to the individual or detriment to society. Such works as Bennet's "Letters to Young Ladies" and Gisborn's "Duties of the Female Sex" were ever in his pocket; works that, in this day of superior light and knowledge, have been rescued from contempt by oblivion.

One day in 1805 he produced his favorite Gisborn and read till mother's patience was almost exhausted. Young as I then was, I wondered it held out so long; but she was a very polite woman. It treated of the natural inferiority of the sex in almost every point of view, and the concluding passage ran thus, " The highest advancement of which she is capable is a dignified marriage." He rested the book on his knee and looked at mother as if he would say, "This is incontrovertible."

She read him Aunt Ruth's essay in reply, observing as she did so, "This is written by a woman whose talents throw Gisborn's entirely in the shade." He made no comment, but it was the last time he brought the book to read to her. So the essay freed her from this petty persecution.

For the *Evening Fire-Side.*

"No more, but hasten to thy task at home,
There guide the spindle and direct the loom."
HECTOR'S *speech to* ANDROMACHE.

"God is thy law, thou mine; to know no more
Is woman's happiest knowledge, and her praise."
MILTON'S *Paradise Lost.*

Such is the language which, from remotest antiquity, has been used by legislators, poets, and philosophers, in order to confine the efforts of the female mind within the narrow limits of household cares.

The assumption and exercise of the privileges of rational and intelligent beings have been withheld from woman by all the jealousy of legislative authority, and forbidden with all the solemnity of religious sanction. But lest the temperate force of reason and the daring powers of genius should overturn the august barriers, the poets also have enlisted in the cause all the charms of harmonious numbers and all the witcheries of Fancy.

Can anything be expected from so powerful a combination but unlimited success? The natural consequence has followed. Accustomed from our earliest infancy to believe that the circumstance of sex has marked out for us a particular path, that neither our sports nor our employments can with propriety be in any degree similar to those of the other sex, we submit our minds to the yoke of perpetual pupilage before we have sufficient penetration to discover the formidable train of consequences to which it will subject us.

The small and imperceptible chains of custom are thrown around us, and, adapting themselves to our growth, become in time too powerful for the utmost efforts of improving reason.

Yet notwithstanding these apparently insurmountable obstacles, some women have dared to think for themselves.

The mounds which the arrogance of man have thrown around the fields of science have, in some instances, given way to the force of truth and the energies of mind. What now is to be done but to change their tactics? The experiment has been made, the powers of the female understanding have been proven. They cannot drive the intruders from the ground thus obtained by the whole thunder of their batteries. But they may deter others from imitating the great example by holding up to ridicule that heroic perseverance which deserves a better recompense.

And hence all their wit and ingenuity have been employed in sketching out the character of learned women. A woman who is conscious of possessing more intellect than is requisite in adjusting the ceremonials of a feast, and who believes she is conforming to the will of the giver by improving the gift, is by the wits of the other sex denominated a learned lady. She is represented as slovenly in person, imperious to her husband, and negligent of her children.

And the scarecrow is employed exactly as the farmer employs his unsightly bundle of rags and straw, to terrify the birds from picking up the precious grain that he wishes to monopolize.

After all this, what man in his sober senses can be astonished to find the majority of women, as they really are, frivolous and volatile, incapable of estimating their own dignity, and indifferent to the best interests of society? Yet notwithstanding the obvious inconsistency of the thing, a writer in your paper comes forward with loud complaints against the sex, that they are gay, fashionable, and trifling; not only indifferent to, but absolutely feel contempt for literary pursuits.

And so, forsooth, after exercising your authority to deter us from all useful acquisitions, and this during the lapse of ages, you now, like spoiled children, insult your bauble and cry because it is good for nothing.

Sterne says, "An insult added to an injury makes every man of sensibility a party." It is this strong sense of injustice that compels me to take up the pen. I am one of the despised sex, and I bear in my bosom a heart swelling with honest indignation at those absurd prejudices which have so often repressed the noble fervors of a generous spirit. From my parents I derived neither beauty to attract, nor affluence to command attention; of course was doomed to pass my life in indolent obscurity. How often, while exulting in that consciousness of intelligence which claims kindred with the wise and good of all ages, while my heart expanded with the warm glow of benevolence, and with ardent wishes to become great and useful, have I sunk into sickening despondence when I reflected on my sex! How often have I cast a despairing eye on those walls which guard the fields of science and the paths of literature from female profanation!

Now, indeed, the balance is inclining in our favor. Our eyes are becoming opened to see that those gentlemen deceive us who tell us that to be beautiful, to move with grace, and to dress with elegance are all we need aspire to. We shall perceive that even these, when the charm of novelty is past, quit with indifference the conversation of those who are not possessed of more substantial accomplishments.

Let us, then, unite in the general cause, the improvement of our understanding. Let us zealously and modestly cultivate our intellectual powers. And while we endeavor to enrich our minds with the knowledge and the firmer virtues which have hitherto been termed masculine, let us not forget to engraft on them those humble duties and those gentle affections that belong to us as women.

ELIZA PICKERING.

I TAKE my pen, probably for the last time, to memorialize a member of the Johnson family, and that one an only and beloved sister. Though our parents had but two daughters, our childhood was not spent together; when almost an infant, she was given to her grandparents at their earnest request, and remained with them until grandmother's death, when she came back to our home, which she left not again till her twenty-fourth year, when she became the wife of Jonathan Pickering, and removed to his farm in Solebury.

After continuing there a few years they settled near Philadelphia, where the remainder of her life was passed. She was very domestic in her habits, and never had a large circle of acquaintance, but by the favored few who possessed her friendship she was warmly beloved, and her attachment to them was of the most unselfish character. Her imperfect hearing during the latter part of her life was, no doubt, one reason for her taking so little interest in general society. But independent of this cause, she always enjoyed the quiet pleasures of home.

> "Joys felt alone, joys asked of none,
>   Which time's and fortune's arrows miss."

She had the talent for painting and poetry that characterized her family, and cultivated both, in her early days. After her marriage her pencil was laid aside, but she indulged her poetic taste till almost the close of life, and published many poems in the periodicals of the day, that were deservedly admired.

I will introduce one or two that appeared in the *Triple Wreath* at the close of this memoir, believing that this manuscript may at some future time meet the eye of those that have never seen that little volume, a small edition of which was printed more than thirty years ago.

I find it more difficult to select from among her poems those to which I would give the preference than of almost any cotemporary female writer, for she never wrote carelessly, and often observed that, as poetry was not a necessity of our nature, but one of its luxuries, it need not be tolerated when below mediocrity. But if not a necessity, it was to her

> " Its own exceeding great reward,
>   Beyond all pleasures dear."

When she was thirteen and I eleven our father engaged a governess to instruct us in our home; the school in the neighborhood at that time not having his approbation.

Our teacher, Ann Thompson, was an English woman, a graduate at York boarding-school, and subsequently a teacher at Acworth, a seminary of equal celebrity.

She united herself with the Society of Friends, and came to this country at the age of twenty-five; among her companions on the voyage were Martha Routh and Charity Cook, both well known public Friends.

Captain Paddock, the owner of the vessel, named it the " Friends' Adventure," as so many of the passengers were members of that society.

Within half a mile of the school she taught lived Lindley Murray, the grammarian and judicious compiler of school-books. Thousands who were pupils the early part of the present century, will acknowledge with me their indebtedness to him for many a lesson of morality and religion : "Bright gems of thought, and golden veins of language." He was a frequent visitor at the school and always a welcome guest, for, beside his pleasant manners and cheerful converse, he made the children large presents of fruit from his ample orchard,—a circumstance doubtless as fully appreciated by them as any part of his visit.

Ann Thompson, some years after, was married to a member of the respected Marriot family up the North River. She was with us a year, the only time and place that my sister and myself attended any school. Our brother, William H. Johnson, was also her pupil; but he completed his education at the boarding-school of Enoch Lewis, in Chester County.

My sister always mentioned that year with delight; the school was limited to twelve students, all females, except brother and our cousin Matthias Hutchinson, our only near relative on the maternal side. They mostly were children of our parents' friends, generally girls of our own age, and those we expected to be our associates in womanhood.

Eliza often gave them the benefit of her poetical vein; several of us tried our hands, but she was ever in advance of us all.

The apple-orchard was our favorite resort in the sultry summer noons; we would seat ourselves among the branches of a tree easy of ascent, and perpetrate what we termed poetry to an indefinite extent, and riddles almost without number; some of these, at seventy-five, come up often vividly before me.

Alas! the tree that was the scene of our blithe songs of glee has long been missing from its place, and few of the joyous beings that sat among its branches now live to tell the tale of that happy olden time.

Another recollection of a pleasant playground is so often in my mind that I will give it a place in this narrative. On my visits to my sister, at our grandfather's rural and not inelegant abode, our favorite stroll was to a retired spot on his premises, used as a graveyard during the Revolutionary war. There, seated on the graves, with our books, was spent many a summer afternoon.

With the history of those who slept beneath those rustic mounds we were, of course, generally unacquainted. There was, however, one exception, for our mother had told us a tale that thrilled our young hearts with sympathy.

The only child of Marinus Willett, and bearing his name, had died at grandfather's during the war, and been buried in this sequestered spot. A few years after he was disinterred and taken to his native place to be deposited in the family vault. Mother distinctly remembered this circumstance, but not the first interment.

He was a fine young officer in the American army, and much lamented. His father was the intimate friend of Lafayette, and the companion of his journey during his last visit through this country. My maternal grandmother, Elizabeth Hutchinson, wrote to the mother of young Willett on the subject of his death and burial. I read the correspondence when a child, and do not recollect having seen it since. Grandmother's portion of it impressed me so permanently, perhaps because in verse, that I could recite most of it in after-years. Now, with the exception of a few lines, they have faded from my memory.

Those lines I will copy, as a relic of the past, for though they lack poetic merit, they were calculated to soothe the anguish of a sorrowing mother,—

> Think not, my friend, he is inglorious laid,
> Without a tear beneath the woodland shade,
> For many a tear bedewed that hallowed tomb
> When in our burial-place we gave him room.
> And not without a friend, for all who knew
> Thy darling son he their attention drew;
> Something too noble for this world below
> Did in each look and every action glow.

Should any, in this more cultivated and progressive age, be disposed to criticise these unpretending elegiac lines, I would remind them that they were written by a country matron over a hundred years ago, in a rural district where literature flourished but little and a very small amount of education was deemed sufficient for a female.

> "To ply the distaff by the twinkling light,
> And to their daily labor add the night,"

was considered at that time a more important accomplishment than to ply the pen, even with superior grace and power.

Elizabeth Hutchinson was, however, far in advance of her neighborhood cotemporaries. Her school learning had probably not been superior, but her fondness for reading had, in a measure, supplied the deficiency, as she was certainly the best-read woman in her section of country.

Letters between her and her stranger friend were occasionally interchanged for years. I remember the last most distinctly of any. It was accompanied by a silver cream-cup. The letter ran thus:

Offer, in my name, this trifling gift to your daughter, now on the eve of marriage. Happy friend, to have a son and daughter to inherit the fruits of your labors, while the only flower that grew in our garden has fallen by untimely blight.

The letter also expressed warm gratitude for their kindness to her son when dying among strangers.

But I will not protract reminiscences that, I am aware, cannot be equally interesting now to any other. Sister of my heart, a long and last adieu.

"Her worth, her warmth of heart, let friendship say,
    Go seek her genius in her living lay."

ELIJAH ON MOUNT HOREB.

BY E. PICKERING.

Alone, on Horeb's sacred mount,
  The seer Elijah stood,
While passed before his wondering sight
  The mighty power of God.
For lo! a sweeping whirlwind rose,
  The quaking rocks it rent,
And fiercely o'er the trembling hills
  Its wrathful course was bent.
Yet spoke not in this tumult wild
  The voice the prophet sought;
That voice, so awful yet so dear,
  No angry tempest brought.

And after came an earthquake dread,
  The shaking earth was riven,
And clouds of dark, sulphurous smoke
  Obscured the light of Heaven;
Then fell the lofty works of men,
  Their towers and temples fair,
And where the once proud city stood
  A whelming flood was there!
Yet not from all this fearful wreck
  Arose that solemn word;
'Twas but the putting forth of power,
  The pathway of the Lord.

Next came a far-consuming fire,
　Majestically bright,
And oh! severely beautiful
　Was that most glorious light.
Wide o'er Samaria's splendid domes
　The glowing radiance streamed,
And Horeb's everlasting rocks
　In flaming grandeur gleamed.
'Twas not of earth that light sublime,
　And yet no word was there;
The word the holy prophet sought
　With humbled soul to hear.

At length a still, small voice was heard;
　Elijah bowed his head,
And o'er his face his mantle's shade
　With silent reverence spread.
Prophetic was that voice divine,
　Of strange events it spoke;
It told that soon a faithless race
　Should wear the Syrian yoke.
And high behests to him it gave,
　Commandments of the Lord;
Then forth the righteous prophet went,
　Obedient to the word.

SUGGESTED BY THE FIRST VIEW OF A COMET.

BY E. PICKERING.

Hail, beautiful stranger! I welcome thy beaming,
Through far depths of ether resplendently gleaming;
All glorious and bright in thy burning career,
I hail thee with reverence, unmingled with fear.

No terrors attend thee, no dread train of fire,
Portending wars, earthquakes, or pestilence dire;
But lovely and calm as the planet of even,
Thou look'st from thy path in the azure of Heaven.

Whence comest thou, fair visitant, where is thy home?
Through what unknown systems or spheres dost thou
    roam?
Does thy lamp, thro' the vast wilds of ether self-borne,
Ever cheer the cold realms of Uranus forlorn?

To mount for a space in thy chariot of fire,
In visions romantic might fancy aspire,
Through the boundless expanse of creation be roll'd,
And glance at the wonders thy course would unfold.

Oh! might we not pass in our limitless range
The wild realms of chaos all formless and strange?
But a glimpse of the homes of the blest could we see?
Are the souls of the guilty imprisoned in thee?

But hence with conjectures as useless as vain ;
Enough we behold thee on Heaven's broad plain,
Enough that wherever thy splendors shall move
To know they are guided by Infinite Love.

TO THE COMET.

WRITTEN AFTER ITS DISAPPEARANCE FROM OUR HEMI-
SPHERE.—E. PICKERING.

Thou hast gone in thy brightness, thou beautiful star,
With the train of refulgence that streamed from thy car,
Where Philosophy's eagle-flight never may soar,
Nor e'en Fancy's bold pinion attempt to explore.

Had the spirit commission'd thy splendors to guide,
If spirit there be—o'er thy course to preside?
But design to commune with some child of the earth,
And pour on his rapt ear the tale of thy birth.

What wonders thought never conceived had been told,
Of magnificence angels alone could behold!
Oh! why, among all who have gazed on thy light,
Was there none ever blest with communings so bright?

When the stars of the morning triumphantly sang,
And the shouts of archangels in joyfulness rang,
Was then thy glad orb launched on ether's vast deep,
Unchanging for ages its pathway to keep?

What spheres has thy lamps' rich effulgency warmed,
'Mong suns, and through systems, unharming, unharmed,
In safety and peace was thy swift career bent,
Or in fearful concussion to rend or be rent?

Was thine the dread task in rude fragments to shiver
Some world like our own, into new worlds to sever?
Such, philosophers tell, might the Asteroids be,—
Do these owe their separate existence to thee?

Ah! little of thee can proud science impart,
To show what thou'st been, or unfold what thou art,
Save that two thousand years she has mark'd thee on high,
And traced thee returning again to the sky.

Speed on, glorious one, in thy wonderful course,
From the beams of our sun gain new light and new force:
Still roll on through ether thy chariot sublime,
Till Eternity springs from the ruins of Time.

THE progress of these biographical sketches now leads me to speak of "the mother that looked on my childhood,"—whose kindness, early, late, and long, is among the recollections that do not grow fainter with the lapse of years; for every remembrance connected with her— and few are those not in some degree thus connected—grows deeper and stronger as life nears its goal.

May not these sacred memories that here seem a part of our being, and constitute so large a portion of our earthly bliss, be one of the delights of that happier sphere,

> " Where the broad record we have writ
>   Is lying open by ?"

My mother on her marriage settled at Elm Grove, and there consequently are my first recollections of her. I often recall her stately step, as I saw her in my early childhood, her hazel eye beaming with intelligence and kindness. If the beauty was somewhat impaired that had distinguished her girlhood, her peculiar grace of manner was never lost, but remained with her even through life's decline; and that refinement of feeling, the joint gift of nature and cultivation, was not an attribute to lose its power, but rather increased as she passed in quietude along towards that world of purity and love to which her feelings already approximated.

I will mention a circumstance that shows the impression she made upon strangers in her seventieth year. A family from Philadelphia who had never seen her settled in our neighborhood. On their first visit to us she came into the parlor to invite them into the room where she usually sat; but I will let them tell their own story.

We expected to see a person borne down with infirmities and years; we knew her age, and that her delicate health had long confined her at home; but what was our surprise to see a lady graceful in person, tall, and very erect, elegant in manner, and whose every look was intelligence. She seemed to us like a beautiful vision.

She was often rallied by her acquaintance on this imputed sylph-like appearance.

She spent her fifteenth winter in Philadelphia, to learn the French language, and every subsequent winter, at least in part, till her marriage.

Her home when there was at Dr. Hutchinson's, her father's brother; his wife was Lydia Biddle, a woman of refinement and mental culture. She moved in a fashionable circle, and was not in membership with Friends, though most of her family belonged to that sect.

Mother's frequent and protracted visits to them introduced her to a much gayer circle of acquaintance than she would have met in her country home. With some of these she retained her intercourse through life, with others it declined from natural causes.

Among these was Dolly Paine, who has since become a part of her country's history. She was then in beauty's first bright glow, a most magnificent-looking woman, and by no means unconscious of the fact. She was then considered very ambitious, and must eventually have been fully gratified. She was intimate with mother's relatives and much at their house.

Dr. Hutchinson chose for his second consort Sidney, sister of Arthur Howell, a woman of beauty and merit. Mother's marriage took place about the same period.

Her gay city associations fortunately did not disqualify her for the niche assigned her by Providence, that of a country matron, with the numerous cares that belong to the position. Though social, she was domestic, and united the thrifty, careful housekeeper with the literary lady; a union at that time deemed almost impossible, but in the present progressive age it excites neither surprise nor comment.

Perhaps the most prominent traits of her character were the attributes Pope petitioned for,—

> " Teach me to feel another's woe,
> To hide the faults I see."

These were undoubtedly possessed by her in no common degree. She was not only gifted to feel deeply for the woes of others, but ever ready to relieve to the utmost of her power. Nor was the latter part of the quotation given less in the line of her daily experience. Of all persons I have ever known she was the most prompt to make allowance for the frailties of erring humanity. I once heard a friend of ours say to her that she was the only person she had ever known that carried to an extreme the doctrine, at least the practice, of non-resistance, for she would not defend herself at the expense of another, when the materials were at hand and the right was obviously on her side.

Our friend took the ground that the course adopted had a tendency to invite aggression. Neither party made a convert, but the impression made on my mind was that there might possibly be an extreme, even in good, and that the claims of justice are paramount even to those of generosity.

I feel forcibly, while writing this memoir, the truth of Cowper's lines,—

"We loved, but not enough,
The gentle hand that reared us."

Perhaps few persons imbued with even ordinary sensibility have not, at some period of life, responded to this sentiment, and the most probable time when their own heads are silvered by the frost of age.

Earnest gratitude rises in my mind that I am enabled, in my seventy-sixth year, to leave for her descendants this faint tribute to the best of mothers.

Her constitution was naturally frail, yet she lived till her seventy-fourth year, with her mental vigor unimpaired and the warmth of her attachments unabated.

Though in common with most who live to old age, she survived the larger number of her cotemporaries, yet some still remain to whom her name is connected with many pleasant memories, and her acts of beneficence are remembered with affection and gratitude.

Mrs. Sigourney says the aged are not always forgotten,—

" When wisdom's crown, so meekly worn,
    Is shrouded 'mid their frosted hair,
And from a younger race withdrawn
    The example they but ill might spare.

" Then think not when the aged die,
    And find a couch in mouldering clay,
That lightly parts the loosened tie,
    And briefly mourned, they pass away."

A DAUGHTER'S TRIBUTE.

Mother beloved, now flown from human ties
To join the holy anthem of the skies,
I would not call thee back to earthly woes
From that blest land of glory and repose,
Though round my heart the tenderest memories throng
Of all thy kindness—early—late—and long.

Mother, be mine that glorious host to join,
Who rest in beams of light and love divine;
Where not a cloud shall dim our radiant way,
Or sad adieus obscure our Heavenly day.
Not golden harps, nor bloom of fadeless flowers,
But perfect love and endless peace be ours.

MATTHIAS HUTCHINSON.

MATTHIAS, son of Randall and Elizabeth Hutchinson, was born in 1744.

His parents were residents of Falls Township, Bucks County. At what time he left the parental roof is unknown to the writer of this brief memorial of his after-life. It was probably in quite early youth, for at the age of twenty-one years he married, in Friends' meeting, Buckingham, Elizabeth, daughter of Thomas and Elizabeth Bye, of that place. The family name of the latter was Ross. She came with her parents from Ireland some years previous to her marriage, and was sister to Thomas Ross, a conspicuous public Friend of that day. She was remarkable as to intellect and, for the period in which she lived, cultivation of mind.

Her daughters were all superior women, and the one chosen by Matthias Hutchinson for his wife, as regards book-knowledge, was superior to them all. She died eighteen years before him. He never formed another matrimonial connection, and subsequently removed to reside with his daughter, wife of Samuel Johnson, of Buckingham, where he died, 1823, aged eighty years.

His mind remained unimpaired to the last, though for several years he labored under physical debility.

It is not my desire to write a eulogy on this excellent and gifted individual, though a plain and true statement of facts relative to his life and character may seem to bear that impress. Yet do we owe it to his memory to say that in every relation in life his conduct was exemplary and praiseworthy.

His natural temperament inclined him to liberality in an unusual degree, and his business talent had placed in his power ample means to gratify what always appeared to be his ruling passion,—the pleasure of relieving suffering and adding to the happiness of others.

Of his public life we can speak in terms of equal commendation, for it will equally bear the strictest scrutiny. Earlier than the meridian of life, almost to what might be termed old age, he held offices of trust in his native county. He was, while a comparatively young man, appointed justice of the peace, and subsequently an associate judge of Bucks County Court, which office he held many years, and resigned in consequence of increasing age and debility, about the time the seat of justice was removed from Newtown to Doylestown. A few years previous to his resignation he had decided to retire from that office, and when the rumor came to the ears of the presiding judge (Bird Wilson), he remarked, "We cannot spare him; he is an ornament and an honor to the bench." That such was the prevailing opinion of him there is plenty of evidence.

His piety was of a practical character; one of the doers of the law whom we are led to believe from Holy Writ are justified in the sight of Heaven.

He was during all his life a steady attender of the meeting of which he was a member as long as his health permitted; after it did not, he spent the hours, when the family were thus assembled, in reading the New Testament.

It was on one of these occasions, while sitting in a state of mental abstraction, having laid aside his book, that a member of the family, who had remained at home, heard him say, in soliloquy, not seeming sensible any person was present, "I have just twenty months to live." When requested to repeat the observation, he appeared not to hear, at least made no response. In a few minutes, however, he added, "Yes, twenty months exactly."

The person sitting by his side made a note of his expressions, and they were completely verified.

After the family returned from meeting, his daughter had a full conversation with him on the subject, and he told her many things relative to his departure; among others, his having had a view of his friends attending his funeral in sleighs. Suffice it to say, not one of his predictions failed in its fulfilment.

As his life was eminently useful and pious, so was his death peaceful and happy.

His granddaughter, Eliza Pickering, who had lived with him from infancy to womanhood, paid the following poetic tribute to his memory:

Ah! this my heart hath treasured well,
  Benevolence refined and warm,—
Could features more distinctly tell
  A loved and venerated form?

For I, long in thy ancient hall,
  Once owned thy kind paternal care;
How changed! each trace hath vanish'd all
  Of love and joy that lingered there.

But thou, a house not made with hands,
  Eternal in the Heavens, is thine,
To join the bright celestial bands,
  In robes of holy light to shine.

I marked thy closing hour serene;
  Calmly declined thy setting sun;
No cloud the sweetly solemn scene
  Obscured, thy righteous task was done.

I neglected to state at the commencement of
these verses that they were suggested by viewing
a likeness of him in her possession.

AN AUTOBIOGRAPHY.

WRITTEN IN THE SPRING OF 1867.

———

By the solicitation of my children I have been induced to call up for them some memories of the past in the form of autobiography. At first I shrunk from the task, for I had always considered it fraught with difficulties. In speaking of ourselves, to say too much or too little seemed inevitable; the first-mentioned error doubtless the most objectionable, and I have often seen it a failure, even when attempted by the gifted and the good; how slight, then, the probability that, with powers limited as mine and a life so uneventful, it could repay a perusal even to the partial eyes of filial affection. A wish to gratify those objects of my love is a powerful reason why I should comply with their request; but perhaps another motive may almost unconsciously actuate me. Most human beings, especially in age, love to live over again scenes they

72

delight to remember, and that once gave to existence its every charm. Should I commit to paper these pleasant reminiscences, it will, of course, be necessary to look more minutely than I have lately done over days gone by, and may possibly gather many a flower that once dotted my pathway, which, though now withered, may, in the estimation of my children at least, retain a portion of their beauty and fragrance.

The first home where I shared "a father's affection, a mother's caress," was Elm Grove, and there the first seven years of my life were passed. Under those beautiful trees of my father's own planting were spent many of my early hours. But I had seldom companions to share my childhood's glee, as my sister lived with our grandparents, and my brother was not old enough to be very companionable.

I suppose many, perhaps most little girls, under such circumstances, would have resorted for amusement to their dolls, but I never took any delight in them. I would rather sit and hear the birds warble through the branches of the elms, or build my play-house by a brook that ran murmuring by our dwelling; in these I seemed to meet a response that dolls could not afford me. Fortunately I learned to read very early, how early I cannot say, for I have no recollection of being taught that delightful art, that has added so much to the enjoyment of my life. Perhaps no person ever had a happier childhood,—it could not be otherwise, with perfect health, a lovely location for a home, and parents as indulgent as judicious training would permit.

They told me in after-life, that in my third year I gave them a lesson they never forgot, and by which they profited. My father had heard a story not very creditable to the parties concerned, and told mother in my presence, not supposing a child so young would understand or remember any part of it; but what their consternation was may be imagined, when, assembled at dinner, I told them I had something "very astonishing" to tell them. Mother tried in vain to divert my attention, and was obliged to bear me from the table and room.

The moral she extracted from this incident was, that more circumspection should be used when speaking before children than is often the case. Few seem aware how early they understand what they hear, and there is certainly much difference in their precocity, even when there is an equal amount of mind.

Seven years soon glided by, and my father purchased a large farm in the vicinity of Elm Grove, and sold that residence to Dr. John Wilson, who was a valuable acquisition to the neighborhood in a social point of view, for he was a man of talent and science, and was also a skilful and popular physician.

The farm we removed to was bounded on one side by Lahaska Mountain, a pleasant and fertile place, which met all our wishes. Father enjoyed his accession of acres, as it gave him a larger sphere in which to exercise his fondness for agricultural pursuits.

As for myself I had but one wish ungratified, a companion to share my pleasures, and by sharing increase them.

My sister, however, lived within two miles of us, and I spent one day in each week with her; my brother, rather more than two years younger than myself, was always the companion of these pedestrian excursions.

Sister came to us comparatively seldom ; grandmother's ill health would not permit her to accompany her, and she was lonely in her absence. Sister, on her part, became so accustomed to the seclusion of a sick-room that it ceased to be irksome.

She was very fond of reading, and grandfather once a week procured for her books from the neighboring library. These she read with much avidity, and when disappointed of a fresh supply, as occasionally would happen, she had recourse to his law library. A young lawyer assured me that her knowledge of "Blackstone" would have been creditable to many of the legal profession.

But this kind of life, with which air and exercise had so little in common, was unfortunate for her in a physical point of view, and might perhaps have laid the foundation of that delicate health which somewhat detracted from life's full enjoyment.

My own situation was as different as possible, for though the principles of physiology were less generally known and spoken of than at present, yet the professors of the science themselves could not have found fault with her practice (I mean mother's), dictated as it was by good sense and observation.

My time was divided between light household employments, study, and rambles among the beautiful scenery our valley affords; these still form some of the brightest pictures on memory's wall.

Wild-flowers of every hue I loved to gather; the honeysuckle and variegated laurel often made our parlor resemble a sylvan lodge; and fern, sweet fern, how often

" When climbing Lahaska in youth's fairy bright dream,
    I've pulled off my bonnet and decked it with thee."

I cannot yet see that plant without emotions of pleasure, as no other revives so many olden memories. Mother was fond of flowers, as her garden manifested, and always greeted my return with my flowery treasure, and never failed to praise my taste in their arrangement, and from her, praise, even on trivial subjects, ever gladdened my heart.

I am aware that these reminiscences may seem trifling in pages claiming to be memories of a life, but for that very reason I think them admissible. Is not life made up of trifles? They weave its web of misery or bliss. Dr. Moore, the traveller, the prince of travellers in my estimation, who was familiar with every view of society, and the inhabitants of almost every clime, when speaking of some amusements of which the Italians are fond, says, "You will term all this trifling, and perhaps it is so; but after the bustling importance some people seem disposed to attach to it, pray, what is human life?"

I have alluded to my studies. In these mother was my preceptor, and a very competent one, especially in grammar, and I commenced school at the head of my class. Reading, too, was my delight, which she always encouraged, but seldom put into my hands books she had not read and approved.

My father had a share in Buckingham Library, which contained many hundred volumes of well-chosen works, but I did not resort to it till I had read and re-read all that our family library contained. It was composed principally of history and biography, with a sprinkling of poetry and one novel only, "The Man of Feeling," which my grandfather brought with him from Ireland.

It was the first fiction I had ever read, and made so deep an impression that, though half a century has elapsed since I saw it, I have as clear a recollection of it as though I had read it yesterday, and lately copied from memory a pastoral from it that I used to recite at nine years old, for the amusement of visitors, and perhaps to gratify parental pride and partiality.

Of historians I preferred Hume, and of the British classics, the *Rambler* and *Adventurer*. I could hardly decide between these, as I considered Hawkesworth the best of all Johnson's imitators,—

"We scarce the pupil from the teacher know."

The *Spectator* I read to mother when I was very young, to improve me in reading. This would now be thought singular; but the world did not then rejoice in works calculated for youthful minds as at present.

Homer's Iliad and Odyssey were among our family volumes, and when reading them, particularly the latter, I seemed to traverse an enchanted land.

With Virgil I was as familiar, but I only read

his poem as sister Eliza read Blackstone, when not supplied with other books, for I considered him a servile imitator of Homer, then my idol. He puts the same dying speeches into the mouth of his fallen heroes, entirely without regard to difference of temperament and character. I know not what abler critics would say, but I was thus impressed by it.

I read about the same time several works of fiction that mother considered would have an elevating effect on the character and aid in forming a correct literary taste.

Conspicuous among these were Evelina and Cecilia. Of the latter the great moralist, Johnson, says, " If you talk of Cecilia, talk on."

Evelina also has much to recommend it. The circumstance of her making her adopted father her confidant of all the perplexities she encountered, when, emerging from the obscurity of his parsonage, she entered fashionable life among the titled and the great, was as remarkable as meritorious, and worthy of imitation.

Richardson's works next came in my way, procured for me by Euphemia Preston, a single woman, many years older than myself, whom I loved very dearly, and who spent several weeks at our house every summer for ten years.

Her acquaintance with books was quite extensive, particularly in this department of literature, and Sir Charles Grandison, whom Cowper calls "the hero and the saint," was completely the hero of her imagination.

It may possibly be termed tedious in this fast age, but its lessons of morality and religion must have had a decided influence for good, appearing at a time when many works in the enticing form of fiction were much read, and were calculated to give very erroneous ideas of life.

History and biography meanwhile were not neglected. Of the latter I was very fond. Johnson's "Lives of the Poets" interested me especially, as, with the claims of truth, they have all the interest that fiction could give, and truth is often stranger than fiction, as well as more instructive.

Then came the mighty magician of the age, Sir Walter Scott,—

> "He who struck old Albion's lyre,
> 'Till round the world its echoes roll."

11

It would be impossible to convey to any one an idea of the electrical effect his poems had upon my feelings at the period of early womanhood, when the taste had acquired considerable maturity and the enthusiasm of earlier days still remained. But thousands have, no doubt, had similar experience. To them all description would be superfluous, and to those who have not, worse than useless, because they could not comprehend it.

The prose works of this author also afforded me much entertainment as well as instruction. I enjoyed them the more for being familiar with the historic facts of which they treat, and the author's fidelity in adhering to those facts greatly adds to their value, as they will generally make a deeper impression, consequently be more permanently remembered than from the pen of the historian.

After my sister came home to reside I began to go into society, as it is termed, and though I read less, my life acquired a new interest from being diversified by mingling with agreeable associates.

Ere I pass to the more important events of my

uneventful life, I will dwell awhile on the days of young romance, for true are the words of the poet,—

"All have had their dreams of joy,
Their own unequalled, pure romance."

I would gladly commemorate, by a passing notice at least, some of those who contributed to the happiness of those early days.

My first warm friendship was formed in child-hood, and continued till death dissolved the tie, after thirty years' duration. Elizabeth Ely, after-ward the wife of Richard Randolph, was con-nected with our family by marriage. Her mother was step-sister to my father, and the nearest ties of kindred could hardly have formed a stronger bond of union than existed between them, or caused a friendship and affec-tion more entire.

They lived in Philadelphia when our intimacy commenced, but she spent a part of every sum-mer in the country, and I passed the greater part of my twelfth winter with her in town. When Elizabeth was fourteen, her father concluded to settle in the country, and purchased of her maternal grandfather his farm near the village of New Hope, on which he had long resided, and to which Uncle Hugh Ely and his family soon removed. The change was probably very pleasant to him and my aunt. They had both been reared in the country, and the latter had returned to the home of her childhood, but Elizabeth felt some regrets, which were shared by her adopted sister and cousin, Hannah M. Canby. Neither had known any home but their city one; of course their attachments were principally centred there.

A letter from Elizabeth, aged thirteen, at the time the removal was first spoken of among them, is at this moment present to my mind, from which I will give an extract, as it manifests the nature of her feelings on the occasion, and is no mean specimen of letter-writing for one of her age and limited practice, as I was at the time her only correspondent.

It would indeed be delightful to be near a friend so beloved as Emilia.* Frequent intercourse might bind those ties stronger than at present unite us. The opportunity

---

* The name by which she knew me as a correspondent.

it will afford to compare views and to read together our favorite authors could hardly fail of such an effect.

Then the beautiful tints that spring and summer landscapes display would invite many a rural ramble, and the variegated hues that autumn unfolds, in their turn would claim our attention. But the dreary aspect of winter does not please me so well. I might possibly be happy with plenty of books, yet how we should miss those social circles that we here enjoy whenever we feel disposed to enter them.

Soon after they were established in their new home she went to Westtown Boarding-School for a year. We corresponded constantly during that period, and her return was quite an era in my life.

We were seldom separated many weeks at one time. We had the same tastes and pursuits, and though we had a large circle of acquaintance, the neighborhood afforded to neither so congenial a friend.

My sister was equally intimate with Hannah M. Canby, her adopted sister. They corresponded constantly till their marriages, which took place within a few weeks of each other. They were then engrossed by new duties and cares, but as their homes were not remote they kept up a friendly intercourse.

Our neighborhood at that day contained many
young people who moved in the same circle, consequently they often met in large companies in
our respective homes. On one of these occasions some thirty of both sexes met at my
father's to spend together a social afternoon.
Among them were our New Hope friends and
Susan Allibone, a beautiful young lady, and not
less celebrated for wit and vivacity.

Soon after the company assembled a subject
was introduced in which all participated, as if
by general consent. Anna Seward's letters had
then just appeared, very amusing and interesting, though critics said they told much that
should not have been told, and I could not help
feeling the justice of the criticism.

But the one read that day in our circle was
liable to no such objection. It is a most graphic
account of a visit she made to the ladies of Lang-
ellen Vale, two young Irish women of rank and
wealth, who had retired from the world and concluded to be satisfied with the society of each
other.

There was much published about them at that
time and the subject discussed in most companies,

for the novelty of it created a sensation. They chose a mountain in Wales for their retreat, and all the appliances that wealth could furnish and taste devise were called into requisition to render it attractive.

Anna Seward had been invited, with a small party of literary friends, to spend a day with them, rather an unusual occurrence, she tells us, as they have to be coy of access, lest their retirement should be too frequently invaded. She describes their dwelling and its owners very minutely. Lady Elinor Butler was more wealthy and intellectual than her friend, Miss Ponsonby, but less beautiful.

I suppose before Dr. Corson had finished the description of the Irish ladies, most persons were reminded of the similarity in appearance between them and our New Hope friends. He told me he thought of it while he was reading, and wondered if we saw the resemblance.

The result was, as might be expected, four of us expressed a wish to make a similar arrangement, and began at once, with the aid of our gentlemen friends present, to fix upon a site on which to erect our edifice. Goat Hill combined more of the features we desired than any other, and was selected.

Dr. Corson cordially approved our decision. We might need a medical attendant, and he would be at hand. Another medical graduate observed the choice we had made would render a consulting physician indispensable, and offered his services.

Susan Allibone, of Philadelphia, was invited to join our little confederacy. She said it was an important movement, and she must consider it well. Having already built several castles in the air, and not finding them answer her expectations, she had learned caution. She was, however, pleased with the general design of the one we had chosen for a model. Its ample library and its Æolian harps ringing with every breeze was quite to her taste; but there was one feature she objected to.

The ladies had invented a machine to manufacture butter, and often prepared it for their own breakfast. Now she had no controversy with the article in question, but it must be served up by other hands. She had lately read of an enchanted castle, whose arrangements pleased her exactly. If we would adopt their system she would gladly unite with us. I only remember the last lines of her description,—

> "The glasses with a wish come nigh,
> And with a wish retire."

Susan Allibone was subsequently mistress of a castle in the very country that these eccentric ladies had retreated from, and I doubt not it answered her expectations.

Wealth and high position do not always confer happiness, but I believe hers was never called in question. She has now left her earthly home for " a home not made with hands."

I have already mentioned the large number of young people our neighborhood at that period contained, and may add, there was among them considerable cultivation. Buckingham Library was open one morning in each week, and was generally crowded by aspirants after knowledge.

Within the last few years I had a letter from a friend whom I had not seen for forty years, he having removed to a distant settlement. It gives so graphic an account of an afternoon spent at my father's in 1813, with a collection

of young people, that I will give an extract
from it.

I have been wandering to-day through the realms of
long ago, and looked over forty years of obliterated time,
and saw you all as you were then, and myself among you
sharing the tranquil joy, the innocent amusements of those
early days, and memory reverts to an afternoon spent in the
hospitable mansion of Samuel Johnson, of Buckingham.

There, by his warm fireside, the aged and the young
met on terms of genuine social familiarity, and there was
canvassed, in high good humor and correct taste, the various merits of the classics, the peculiar excellence and com-
parative worth in literature of Johnson, Addison, Thomson, Milton, and Cowper. All these passed in succession
under strict but fair and liberal criticism, also the value,
beauty, and truthfulness of history, ancient and modern.
And, when the tea-things were removed, a quiet evening
walk closed this pleasant and tranquil day.

In 1814 my sister married and settled in Solebury, about four miles distant from our home;
after that event I spent a large portion of my
time with her, her health being very delicate the
first year of her wedded life.

Her new abiding place was a pretty but retired
location, and no dwelling was visible from its
windows. It was once the residence of her hus-

band's parents, and a large family of children,—
several sons and three beautiful daughters. The
father had died previous to sister going there;
the daughters were all married, and the family
dispersed.

I was happy in my sister's home, but it was a
determined act of the will to be so, for I hardly
dared think of the pleasures I had left in the
dear parental dwelling, and mother's loneliness
was ever before my eyes.

But she was the most unselfish of women,
and willing to make the sacrifice to promote a
daughter's comfort.

An incident occurred while with them calculated to test my presence of mind. My sister
and her husband were making a visit to relatives
in a distant part of the county, and left myself
and the girl in their employ the sole occupants
of the house, except their son about two years
old. In looking back to this event I am rather
surprised they did not procure some one to remain with me, but I cannot recollect that such
a precaution was ever spoken of; had I possessed the timidity not very unusual to my sex
and age, and made the suggestion, it would have

been acted upon at once, but the idea of fear never crossed my mind.

At the usual hour I retired to rest with my little nephew, in the room where my sister usually slept, down-stairs. It opened on to a piazza, the door only secured by a frail bolt, very insecure as a fastening. I left the lamp burning in the Franklin stove, having always had faith in light to keep away intruders; but in the present case it proved unavailing,—no doubt because they knew our defenceless position.

I had been in bed but a few minutes, when the door was fiercely rattled, and I hastily retreated from the room, first dressing myself in my brother-in-law's clothes, even to the hat and overcoat for more perfect disguise, and ran up-stairs to call the girl. I spent no time in telling her my plan, as I knew she would implicitly obey me. I raked out the embers that I had covered up in the large kitchen fireplace; made just enough light to discover two persons sitting there in close proximity.

We had not thus sat long, when we heard the tramp of feet at a window near where we were seated, as it had neither shutters nor curtains. I moved further behind the broad chimney jamb, so that only my hat and arm over Betty's chair were visible.

Our faithful dog warned us that they lingered long around the house, perhaps hoping that Betty's wooer would leave the premises; but finding he did not, they concluded to vacate them, and I knew when they did so, by the barking of the dog indistinctly heard in the distance.

I felt, however, little inclined for repose, and kept my station by the fire. Of her whom chance made the subordinate actor in this little domestic drama and the sharer of my midnight vigil, I may be allowed to say a few words; for on that occasion even her very want of intelligence was useful to me. Nature, as if to compensate for her parsimony in brain, had given her extensive physical developments, and I never think of her without being reminded of Washington Irving's account of the Tripolitan captive and his favorite wife, Fatima, whom he bought by the hundred weight, and had trundled home on a wheelbarrow.

The amusement she derived from the matter was perhaps the novelty of her situation, never having had in her life so long a *tête-à-tête* with the wearer of a hat and coat, and no doubt viewed this " as a type and a shadow," etc.

Sister lived in this home about seven years, but eventually settled near Germantown, where she closed her life. Though separated for many years, the intercourse was constantly maintained by aid of the pen. Seldom more than a week passed without a letter from her and full of interest, even to strangers.

The latter part of her life she lived with her son, and spent most of her time in reading. She kept me informed as to all the works she read, and seldom failed to give an opinion of their merits, and her criticisms were liberal and just.

I will copy a letter written within the last year of her life, which I think will be read with much interest :

1854.

MY DEAR SISTER,—Though I cannot help believing there is a letter on the way for me, I will begin one, and may receive thine ere I close it. I want much to hear of the last departure from the dear old homestead; it was invested with no peculiar charms of situation, but how many associations of the past have endeared it as hardly any other place could be, for there was passed the period

of life generally esteemed the happiest, certainly the most
joyous with me. From thence come the most thrilling
recollections of our dear mother's kindness, years of ease
and social enjoyment under her sheltering wing, so lovingly outspread; and then again when I needed it yet
more at a separate home, so devotedly given. There our
dear old grandfather passed away so peacefully and
sweetly, in such soothing transition, that all the unusual
pangs of parting seemed softened,—none of that harsh
recalling to earth, alas! too frequent, to hinder our upward
gaze.

How I love to think over all these memories, but I
would not live them over again, oh, no! There were enjoyments that are forever gone, hopes that are dead, sorrows that have furled upward like the storm-cloud, who
would wake any of them again? No, let our watchword
be onward, and may we see above them all bright glimpses
of a better home,—so be it, saith my soul, in an earn-
estness of hope and trust.

I have not been from home much this winter, and begin to weary a little of confinement; somewhat relieved,
however, by some pleasant walks in the adjacent woodlands. I look forward to the deliciousness of spring with
all its charm of greenery and flowers, I really think with
more intense delight than I ever did, and I have this
privilege by the right of descent, for both father and
mother had an exquisite relish for rural pleasures.

We have lately had a good deal of amusing reading.
My son has been getting for our library, in his capacity

as director, many new books, which I think will please generally. The lives of Madame de Staël and Madame Roland I have read for the second time, and still find them interesting.

Biography of both by Mrs. Child, and one of her best works.

Then we have read "Roughing in the Bush," by Mrs. Moodie, a sister of Agnes Strickland—that alone would insure it an eager perusal. Yet we could not but feel for a member of an accomplished and literary family, going into the very heart of the wilderness, subjected to all its hardships, with her sensibilities refined by early culture so at variance with her future lot. It made me uncomfortable to think of it, with all the entertainment derived from the book.

Mrs. Moodie is a firm believer in the influence of mind over mind, in a sympathetic mental or spiritual attraction, by which we are made partakers, through invisible space, of the joys and sorrows of another. Her views on this subject do not differ materially from my own, for I have always wondered that the doctrine of spiritual communion is deemed by many so absurd. I mean the main fact that it involves, of a continued interest in those they loved on earth by its departed ones.

I suspect there are not many poets since Milton sung the "Millions of happy spirits," that he tells us, "Surround us, both when we wake and when we sleep," but what have avowed the same belief. For instance, Longfellow's "Voices of the Night," and his last poem, "Phantoms," is full of it.

"The spirit-world, around our world of sense, floats like an atmosphere."

I really was not aware, till lately, when looking over
many hundred pieces of poetry in my possession, how
much this prevailing tint, like " Faith touching all things
with hues of Heaven," is the o'ermastering one where the
dead are referred to.

But my letter is already long, and I turn from this
inexhaustible theme, which has ever been, and will probably be a mystery still, till our vision is cleared in the
land of realities to which we are hastening.   E. P.

In connection with my sister's views, I am
reminded of these lines of Whittier,—

> " 'Tis well for us all some sweet hope lies
> Deeply buried from human eyes,
> · And in the hereafter angels may
> Roll the stone from its grave away."

I will transcribe another letter addressed to a
young friend of hers who had recently lost his
wife, and had occasionally appeared in the min-
istry. It is of an earlier date than the one to
myself that I have just copied.

TO ——.

In every line with truth and feeling penned,
Of one my heart has fondly owned a friend:
A corresponding feeling I could trace,
As the clear mirror answereth face to face.
Whether for loveliness that now no more
Shall on thy path the light of beauty pour,
Gladd'ning its sphere with softly radiant glow,
Thy full heart poured the manly plaint of woe.
Yet still I trust, resigned to Him whose power
Hath borne in safety thro' the afflictive hour.
Whether in solemn thought thy humbled soul
Traced the vast mind that rules the mighty whole
In each event of life's yet early day,
Pointing thy path and marshaling thy way,
My mind with sympathy responsive saw
Each truth, each trial in His holy law:
Could see, as thou hast seen, the wise design
Of Him who judgment "layeth to the line,"
And righteousness unto the plummet brings,—
For not at random move the meanest things;
Much less those higher dispensations given
To lead triumphant to the crowns of Heaven.
Be thine a worthier conflict—nobler one,
Than some who gird the sacred armor on;
Who move too oft where worldly honor calls,
Unfaithful watchers upon Zion's walls.

Forgive this caution, well thy heart I know,
Too pure, too lofty, e'er to fall so low;—
But, oh! what trials press on every state
The injunction needed oft to watch and wait;
And I would have thee clearly shine afar,
With Heaven's own beam, a bright, peculiar star.
Look now around thee, countless fields are white
With harvests ripening in the glorious light
Of that bright Sun that marks us out our day,—
Then labor thou while shines his faithful ray;
And as a leaf or feather in the breeze,
Moved by His will, seek only Him to please.
For soon, how soon, will all earth's pageants fly,
And days that now seem distant far, be nigh.
The ground seems sliding from our weary feet,
And fearful sounds our startled senses greet;
A warning voice in every breeze proclaimed,
Of talents lent, of stewardship reclaimed.
To my beloved young friend the five are given,
Oh, freely dedicate them all to Heaven.
Though I but useless and unworthy prove,
The cause, the soldiers of the Cross I love;
The cause that calls within its Heavenly band,
From every kindred and from every land
Its champions true,—to bravely onward bear
The standard high, and all its perils share.
Farewell, be true and faithful to the end,
So fervent prays thy relative and friend.   E. P.

A few months previous to sister's death she
made us her last visit, and asked us to accompany her to her first wedded home, which she
had not seen since she left it, thirty years before.
We accordingly spent a morning there.

It was changed, as might be supposed, from
the lapse of years, but less than she expected to
find it, as it had passed into many hands since
she had called it home. As she walked with us
over the premises, my husband observed to me,
" She does not incline to converse, it must seem
to her like walking in dreamland, and we will
not interrupt her musings."

She gathered leaves from the shrubbery as
mementos, and we heard her repeat to herself
these appropriate verses :

" This vale was termed happy, its graces have perish'd,
    The thrush builds her nest in its thicket of briers ;
Yet beauty once graced it, the hand of taste cherished,
    'Twas hallowed by friendship and love's gentle fires.
Every flower of the field, every leaf of the wildwood,
    Seems dim to my eye, though unaltered in hue :
Rapture but lies in the magic of childhood,
    And the tales of young hope are as sweet as untrue."

During the interval between this visit and her

Thomas Paxton

death she often spoke of the satisfaction afforded
her by the retrospection. She died in her sixty-
fourth year, and I believe had not from youth to
age a single enemy.

Time moves on, and naught can stay its onward progress. I may now record an event to
me of all others the most important. In the
winter of 1817 I made a month's visit to Philadelphia in company with my friend Elizabeth
Ely, and there met with the person destined to
be my companion through the remainder of
life's devious journey.

In the Tenth month of the same year we
were united in the sacred bands of matrimony.
It was as delightful a day as ever dawned on
young and happy human hearts.

Our families had long been intimate, two con-
nections of the kind had already taken place
among its members, both of which had proved
eminently happy.

My bridesmaids were Elizabeth Ely, of New
Hope, and Sidney Coates, of Philadelphia. I
will not enter into a minute description of our
wedding, as such details have generally been
failures from the days of Sir Charles Grandison

down to the present; I might, were I to give my imagination full scope, say,—

> "There was now such a concourse of beauty and grace,
> As had not since Eden appeared in one place."

But this might possibly be more poetical than true, for such has no doubt often been the opinion of the actors in this incident of life's great drama from time immemorial.

Before I leave the subject I will mention a circumstance that was much spoken of at the time as remarkable.

A public Friend, who happened to be at our monthly meeting when the overseers made their report respecting our wedding, arose and said, "I know nothing of the parties in this marriage, but I feel constrained to say it was by Divine appointment."

I have never had reason to impugn the correctness of his conclusion, which no outward knowledge had induced him to form.

While writing the above page I remembered Charles Miner's observation about weddings. He says, "The account of them is always interesting, and it is impossible to tell who they will not interest." To those who may be of a similar opinion, I will make amends for my brief notice of ours by copying a dream I had many years after. It gives probably as correct a version of the matter as could well be done in so limited a space.

A DREAM OF REALITIES.

We met in yonder city's throng,
　In life's bright morn of hope and glee;
But ne'er can memory tell, nor song,
　Of all that meeting brought to me.

Of visits to my quiet home,
　Its cultured lawn and flowery dell,
Of many a devious ramble there,
　Lahaska's wooded vale might tell.

At length a social group convened
　Within my girlhood's happy home;
And plighted hearts and hands were joined
　In that old dear parental dome.

'Twas Autumn in her loveliest mood,
　The sunlight streamed o'er hill and plain;
Lahaska's summit might have seen
　Ascend a youthful bridal train.

No thought what changing years might bring
 O'er festive joys could cast a gloom;
The very breath of Heaven to them
 Seemed fraught with music and perfume.

Now threescore years and ten have flown,
 And children's children fair I see;
Yet still will memory linger long
 · On all that meeting brought to me.

I remained at my father's the winter succeeding our marriage, as we went to reside at my husband's parental home at Abington, and his father did not relinquish housekeeping till spring. My brother at this period married my husband's youngest sister, and took her to the home I had left; two other sisters had settled a few months previous, making four of the family that had married in less than a year.

I found my Abington home altogether agreeable, an elder brother, Jonathan Paxson, living with us, having a grist-mill on the premises.

This formed one of the many pleasant features of our new establishment. He was a man of talents and information, very kind in disposition, and cheerful in temperament.

Three younger brothers also were often with us, all well calculated to contribute their share in forming the delightful atmosphere that pervaded the home circle.

But the most agreeable feature of all, when my husband was not concerned, was the presence of my father-in-law, Jacob Paxson, who lived with us as long as we remained at that place. He was more than seventy years of age, but bright and genial as in early manhood, and as companionable to me as if no difference of age had existed between us.

He was conversant with many of my favorite authors, and having reared a very large family of children, his experience of life's many cares and absorbing duties was of course extensive. His mind was stored with practical truths, and his fund of anecdote seemed inexhaustible.

He had some years before gone to Canada under an appointment from the Yearly Meeting, to establish meetings there. Many an incident connected with that journey he detailed for my amusement and instruction, and he had the happy faculty of blending both in his narratives. In short, he supplied in a greater degree

14

than I had supposed possible the familiar intercourse I had enjoyed beneath the parental roof.

I had much pleasure, too, in the neighborhood associations; many were intelligent, and
all attentive and kind; the intimacies I formed
there were mostly with my seniors in age, and
they have now gone to their reward. I know of
hardly one of this class remaining.

Martha Foulke, formerly Shoemaker, still
lives, though she feels the weight of infirmities
and years. I spent two days with her in the
interchange of olden memories last summer;
neither will, I trust, forget that meeting, probably our last on earth.

Our sister, Sarah Tyson, lived within a few
miles of us. She was all kindness, indeed, there
seemed no other ingredient in her composition.
She was then surrounded by a large family of
young children, for whom her hopes have been
realized, as they are useful and respected members of the community.

We remained a year at Abington; at the
expiration of which father Paxson purchased a
farm in Buckingham, since known as Walnut
Grove, to which we removed in 1819; it was

within a mile of Elm Grove, my native home, and less than two from my father's residence.

This revival of former associations I found very agreeable, and to be again a member of the meeting I had attended from my earliest recollections was not a small item among the pleasant things afforded by my change of residence.

Samuel Johnson Paxson, our eldest child, was three months old when we came back to the scenes of my early youth.

Though our quiet life in our rural home did not furnish much that may compensate for the recording, or may interest after the lapse of years, yet it was not devoid of interest to us at the time; of daily duties conscientiously performed the reward is certain.

The first three summers spent on our Buckingham farm were seasons of unusual drouth,—two of them beyond any we have known before or since,—and, though discouraging, we only shared the common lot, and looked forward to brighter days, which in due time came.

Then we always had our full share of life's best treasures,—

" Joys that riches ne'er can buy,
    And joys the very best."

Of social and domestic pleasures we had ever
an ample share, and the proximity to my parents'
dwelling added much to my life's full enjoyment.
My maternal grandfather, whose home was with
them, closed his life in 1822. But little other
change that concerned us at least took place in
the immediate neighborhood, except that we
purchased, in 1823, the farm on which we resided, and made improvements that rendered it
an unusually attractive and pleasant home. The
situation was beautiful. In front was a meadow
interspersed with wild-flowers of every hue, behind it

" A wood that, half hiding a cottage, would bring
    All the bright hues of autumn, the freshness of spring."

A clear brook ran by the door, adding much
to the beauty and still more to the convenience
of the place.

My retrospections as regard that location are
mingled with kindly memories. It was our
happy home for twenty-six years, and dearer to
me for being my children's first abiding-place.

" For there, beneath its towering, ample shade,
  Three cherub forms of infancy have played ;
  Who fondly still in after-years recall
  The mimic water-wheel and bounding ball."

There is an idea very prevalent in the world
that more difficulty and responsibility exists in
bringing up a family of sons than of daughters.
I have heard the sentiment advanced all my life,
and gave it a certain amount of credence, but I
am glad to say never realized it, for our sons
never discovered any disposition to mingle with
unsuitable society, but always appreciated home
pleasures.

Perhaps a fondness for reading, early in life
cultivated, had a tendency to bring about this
result. Boys, in many neighborhoods, are suffered to spend their leisure hours, and particularly on First day afternoons, in roaming over
the country in companies together, and often
much evil results from these associations. Many
parents commit a serious error in not procuring
works calculated to interest the unfolding minds
of children.

Differently constituted minds, too, require different aliment. I remember once several of our

boys' schoolmates came to spend the afternoon with them. They all went out to play, but one of them was soon among the missing. Many inquiries were made of me respecting him, but I could give them no information. Late in the afternoon, going into his room, I found him seated at his desk with the large Bible spread open before him, in the contents of which he seemed much absorbed. "Mother, don't tell them where I am," he exclaimed, on my entrance, and I kept his secret. He was quite as social in his nature as his brothers, but in this instance he gave up a smaller pleasure to enjoy a greater.

They became interested very early in botany and mineralogy, which opened another avenue in which to spend profitable leisure hours.

The two youngest made a little excursion one summer to Schooley's Mountain, Budd Lake, and Mauch Chunk. At the latter place they met some particular friends from Philadelphia, which was a large addition to their pleasure while there. After an absence of a week they returned to gladden our hearts, with their cup of enjoyment overflowing and their carriage laden with mineral treasures.

Before we had passed many years at Walnut Grove a circumstance occurred that increased for many years our social pleasures. Dr. Wilson, who purchased Elm Grove of my father, married the widow Mary Fell, whose family name was Gillingham. Her mother and mine were relatives, and had been intimate in girlhood; but with her, until her last marriage, I was but slightly acquainted. Our intercourse was frequent after she became the wife of our physician and friend. She was a superior woman, of engaging manners and a cultivated mind.

She brought with her to Elm Grove a son and a daughter. The son, J. Gillingham Fell, of Philadelphia, is well known for his many acts of munificence, being resolved, as appears, that the public should reap the benefit of his almost unexampled prosperity.

The daughter, Phebe Ann Wright, now of Wilkesbarre, has been a correspondent of mine ever since her thirteenth year. It commenced when she was at Burlington Boarding-School, and has continued down to the time in which I write. I am older than her mother, and suppose friendships between persons of such dissimilar ages are not usual, and where there is less inequality they are not always so permanent. Be that as it may, ours has survived all changes through, unbroken by time and unshaken by absence.

She was very remarkable for early maturity. At thirteen she would pass creditably, as regards intellectual culture, for five years older. Her reading was extensive and diversified. She was fond of poetry, and her taste in it was exquisite, yet have I seen her at twelve years old quite engrossed by a work of controversial theology.

In my retrospect of the past I do not find, in all our long and familiar intercourse, one blot to mar the beautiful picture of memory.

After the death of Dr. Wilson and the removal of his family to Doylestown, John Magoffin, of Philadelphia, became the possessor of Elm Grove. His family consisted of a wife and sister, all of them past the meridian of life. They were a great acquisition to our neighborhood in every respect, for they were intelligent and cultivated as well as of large benevolence, and what does not often happen, or rather not always, had the means of indulging that amiable propensity, much to the benefit of their poorer neighbors.

He had been a Presbyterian minister several years, but on account of some conscientious scruples had, a short time before he settled among us, sent in his resignation, and was no longer a member of that sect. His wife and sister both remained members, but not of the same division of the society, the wife belonging to the New School, the sister to the Old, thus presenting the perhaps unusual case of the only three composing a family being of different religious creeds. He, however, steadily attended church with them, and often held meetings on Sabbath afternoons in private families, discovering much interest and zeal that his hearers should embrace the only enduring good, the one thing needful, pointing them less to creeds and doctrines than to practical righteousness.

The first visit I made them was in company with my son Edward, then a youth of twelve. Our host took us into his library, where he had engravings of sixty of the ancient reformers.

Edward examined them with intense interest; he had read a good deal respecting them, and we are always interested in seeing the countenances of those of whom we have historical knowledge. I thought the aspect of many of them very forbidding; but I recollected that they had much to arouse their combativeness. Our friend said to us on that occasion, "I consider George Fox the best of all the reformers."

I became soon intimate with them, which was probably increased by his discovery that I was willing to aid him in carrying out his numerous and various plans of benevolence. I knew the neighborhood well, and he was comparatively a stranger, and I often went round to collect money for some charitable object he had in view.

I remember a ramble taken in Lahaska Valley for that purpose, and when I returned to his house to tea I had the pleasure of presenting him with more than sixty dollars I had collected, —a favorable comment on the liberality of the inhabitants.

They lived ten years in that place, then removed to Bristol. He has now gone to his reward, which was, I doubt not, sure. His sister

Mary preceded him to the grave. Cornelia, his widow, still lives; she was many years younger than her husband.

I will now speak of a delightful era of my life. In 1830 my parents came to reside with us permanently, as regards their earthly sojourn. Father was with us thirteen years before he "ended his pilgrimage and began his life;" and mother ten years ere she passed to a better inheritance.

Such a change had long been in anticipation, especially as mother's frail health rendered the cares of house-keeping burdensome. Father, of course, felt fewer of the inconveniences of their position, and had besides the strongest local attachments that I have ever known. In the place that had been their home for thirty years these interests were concentrated; he had done much to improve and render the property a desirable abiding place.

But he saw the propriety, as well as necessity, of giving up cares that press heavily on age, and I was glad to see how very soon he became entirely at home in his new residence. Some months after they settled there I received a poetical letter from sister Eliza alluding to that event, from which I make the following extract:

Now gayly my fleet little messenger wend
Where graces and virtues harmoniously blend,
Where wreathed in her own glowing fancies so bright
The Muse hovers round in her mantle of light.
Maternal affection still tender and true,
The virtues her poet so gracefully drew;
A sister's warm heart ever cheerful and kind,
To worth most substantial, now happily joined.
And now let me join in thanksgiving and praise
To the power that crowns with His goodness our days,
For the blessings dear father describes as surrounding
His dwelling, with heartfelt enjoyments abounding.
Long, long, be such pleasures his pathway to crown,
Till his sun in calm brightness serenely goes down.

About the time our parents came to our home Hannah Lloyd and her sister, Martha Hampton, established a boarding-school for girls in the village of Greenville. A day-school, where both sexes were admitted, was also part of the establishment; this our two youngest sons attended.

We had a great deal of young society in consequence of the proximity of the seminary.

Many of the pupils were the daughters of our friends in different sections of the country, and of course visited us; seldom more than two weeks passed by without a little company of them taking tea with us.

This was especially agreeable to the girls confined all the week in close study, and was also pleasant to us, not merely because it is ever a pleasure to mingle with fresh young minds, but from the hope of being useful to them by the association.

Father, and mother too, enjoyed these social meetings, and he frequently gratified them by writing original poetry in albums. In less than two years he wrote in a hundred of these books, and I often meet with them yet on centre-tables where I visit.

Among the pupils most intimate at our house was Matilda Powell, now the admired wife of Stephen Rushmore, of Long Island. She sometimes, when engaged in drawing, would obtain permission to spend the day with me in company with a schoolmate with whom she was intimate, and was engaged in the same branch of study; this was my niece, Jane Johnson. They found the quiet of our parlor more congenial than the crowded school-room. Matilda was then sixteen, and remarkably intelligent and companionable. Many years after I received from her a letter, of which I give the following extract:

Many thanks, my dear friend, for thy kind letter, which served not only as a sweet remembrance of one with whom I should be happy much oftener to hold converse, but it also communicated to my heart an electric spark caught from the fires that lit up life's early morning.

Then came, oh! so peacefully in living beauty, those dear images of the past, the loved, the lost of heart's best treasures, now clothed in light, and their countenances illumed with spiritual joy,—they left us in tears, but they come back and find us rejoicing. I can never forget how pleasant were those scenes of my girlhood, when thou wast so kind a partaker of my juvenile pleasures, with the dear ones then around thee.

I trust these precious memories will ever remain, as their tendency is calculated to calm and elevate the soul.

The sweet lines* thee sent me were truly poetical, and I am informed quite appropriate in their application, and I doubt it not, yet I think them really descriptive of

---

* The Three Brides.

the author's self,—of her own warm fancy and overflowing heart.

I rejoice, my dear friend, that thy life is enriched with treasures thou art so well prepared to appreciate. But come to us with thy husband,—we, too, have of life's best riches,—come, and let us talk of life, and how with us has been its gradual unfoldings. Our favorite Swedish author calls all life's changes but the perfecting of our being,—such it should be, and no doubt is, when the soul is brought into harmony with the Divine mind and stands revealed a spiritual being.

Not far from the period I have been writing of a circumstance occurred which, though it might not be classed among important events at the time, was fraught with interesting consequences for a length of years, and still we experience a measure of its benign influence.

Thomas undertook the guardianship of two young girls, Martha and Ruth Beans. They were neighbors, and their mother my relative on the maternal side. There had been no particular intimacy between the families till my husband accepted that office, which of course induced much intercourse and established a warm and lasting friendship.

Ruth, the youngest, was at one time a year

with us. She came to make a few weeks' visit, but being then not in very good health, and being very happy there, we prevailed on her to make a more protracted stay. We found her companionable and became fond of her, a feeling we knew was perfectly reciprocal. She died in early life. Rachel, her eldest sister, married and settled at New Brighton. Mary and Martha still live with their aged and infirm mother in Philadelphia, a bright example of filial affection and many other virtues.

For several years, in what seems now the "long ago," anti-slavery and temperance lectures were of frequent occurrence in our neighborhood. They were generally held in the school-house on the meeting premises. The first one of the former class that I ever attended was delivered by Arnold Buffom, one of the twelve who held the first meeting under the new organization, in an obscure garret in Boston.

He told us in his lecture that he fully believed there were those present that would see the utter downfall of slavery. Few of his audience, I suspect, had much confidence in the prediction. I acknowledge I had not. Yet there are, I know, several still living that were present on that occasion. To these how significant those beautiful lines of Whittier:

> " Did we dare, in our agony of prayer,
>   Ask for more than he has done?
>   When was ever his right hand,
>   Over any time or land,
>   Stretched as now beneath the sun?
>
> " How they pale, ancient myth and song and tale,
>   In this wonder of our days;
>   When the cruel rod of war
>   Blossoms white with righteous law,
>   And the wrath of men is praise."

Temperance lectures, too, were not less frequent. Many gifted men came among us for that purpose, and had large and attentive audiences, and there was an evidence of improvement and reformation in many instances.

I had never, till this period of my life, heard a temperance lecture. My mother was a practical temperance woman, but the subject was at that time rarely discussed, even in the home-circle. An incident occurred when I was ten or eleven years old that probably impressed me more than a dozen lectures could have done. Mother had a present of a bottle of cordial from a friend in town, and shortly after, what was my childish amazement to see her seat herself on the door-step and pour it on the ground. I ran to her, attracted by the agreeable odor, exclaiming, "Oh, mother, let me take it to the harvesters." She replied, "That would be no better than drinking it myself, as it might nourish in them a taste as lasting as ruinous."

The temperance era was also the one when Lyceums flourished in our neighborhood. They were sometimes held in the school-house, but oftener in the houses of the members, where the location was convenient.

The boarding-school was frequently opened for the purpose, and there were often more than fifty persons collected, generally members, and much interest as well as usefulness was the result. Very young persons participated in the exercises of the meetings, some of them taking a conspicuous as well as creditable part.

In course of time the boarding-school was relinquished, and of the most prominent individuals that composed the lyceum, many of the females married and settled in other locations, and the young men engaged in business in different parts of the country.

The last meeting the society held was attended by Dr. Brevoort, of Philadelphia, a phrenologist. It was very large, as he had been invited to attend, and was expected to speak, which privilege he exercised till some of the members were tired of the entertainment. One of our youngest members, a youth of fourteen, noticed the matter in the form of an obituary, and sent it to our county paper. It was thus introduced to the public by the editor:

We insert the following communication, taking it for granted its statements are true, as a member makes them.

We feel sorry that the lyceum, like other children of genius, was too precocious for a long life, or, as it is said, "too smart to live long," and are surprised that phrenology should have been permitted to bump it to death while in such a weak state.

" *Obituary.*

" Died at Buckingham School-house, of lingering decline, Second month, 1839, the Buckingham Lyceum.

"It has seldom fallen to our lot to record a death which has cast so deep a gloom over the social circle. Its patience during the long illness that terminated its life, its mild and salutary rules of discipline, its funds of pleasure and improvement, together with the ardent zeal of its members, have all conspired to entwine it deeply in the hearts of the lovers of literature and science. The spring preceding the past winter its decline evidently progressed, and upon winter setting in its members were obliged to give up every vestige of hope. Everything that medical aid could effect was done by its physician, but without success. In this extremity it was concluded to send for Dr. Brevoort, of Philadelphia, in hope that his great skill might be of some use in so critical an emergency. He came, but not understanding the case exactly, administered too heavy a dose, from which the patient never recovered.

"Some attempts were made to resuscitate it, but the vital spark had fled, and nothing now remains of that once proud society but its name, which, I trust, will ever live in the hearts of those who were its warmest supporters.

"A MEMBER."

In the spring of 1840 our eldest son, Samuel J. Paxson, married Mary Anna Broadhurst, and commenced farming in the neighborhood. During the same summer his brother, Edward, entered the office of the *Village Record*, in West Chester, to acquire a practical knowledge of the printing business. There he remained two years. He then published the *Newtown Journal*, a paper principally devoted to literature, and neutral in politics, in the charge of which his eldest brother united. They continued it several years with credit and success, then chose other locations. Edward established the *Daily News* in Philadelphia, and S. J. Paxson published a paper in his native county, which he continued till failing health warned him to seek the ease and quiet of his pleasant country home.

Edward soon resigned the editorial chair for the legal profession, for which he had, from very early life, a strong predilection, and in which he still remains.

In the winter of 1840 mother was removed by death. Father remained with us three years longer. After mother's death he solaced his loneliness with his books. I heard him say that he read two hundred pages a day on an average.

Mother's departure was sudden, notwithstanding her many years of delicate health. Father's sickness was more protracted, though he had seldom been confined to the house, even for a day. He retained to the last his consciousness and perfect serenity of mind.

" No cloud dimmed their sunset while sinking to rest,
  Bright glimpses they caught of the realms of the blest;

Yet what grief thrilled our hearts, and what tears filled
　our eyes,
As they passed from that home to their home in the skies."

Soon after father's death we removed to the
farm on which we reside at present, and called
Woodlawn, near Lahaska Mountain. It is part
of the farm on which twenty years of my life
were passed. Our son, Albert, had, in 1844,
married Mercy, daughter of Dr. Beans, of Solebury, and to them we resigned Walnut Grove,
and erected for ourselves buildings on our new
purchase in 1845 and 1846.

Edward M. Paxson has now become the
possessor of this property, and is improving
and beautifying it, but it is still our home as
heretofore.

About the time we contemplated a removal
to this place I had a letter from my friend,
Hannah Townsend, of Philadelphia. She is
now no more in this state of being, but her
memory is fondly cherished by many attached
friends. She made us many a visit at Walnut
Grove, and lived to see us pleasantly settled here
at Woodlawn.

When we came near home, on returning from

our rides, she used to say, "Oh! that beautiful white cottage leaning against the mountain."

One of the last two weeks of her life was spent with us. She died a few days after her return home. We passed that week in copying for the press her "History of England in Rhyme." She said to me, as we sat together at the work, "If I am mother to the book, thee is its grandmother, as thee made the suggestion, without which I should not probably have thought of it."

I will make an extract from the letter she wrote to us on our change of residence:

We sat at eventide, and I
  Discoursed, as best I may,
Of you, your characters, your home,
  And how beneath your sway
All feel it is a happy reign,
And if they leave, return again.

Of thy employments, too, I spoke,
  Thy cellar and thy dairy;
Thy coloring for the world around,
  Thy shirt-making—till Mary
Declared it was a shame for me
That I had left my book with thee.

Soon after this the book returned.
  Now, thought I, "here's a letter."
I opened it, but none appeared ;
  I shook the leaves,—no better
Success attended than before,—
I turned the pages o'er and o'er.

But all in vain, for it had come,
  Without a word to say,
That freshly in your memory
  I live from day to day.
And though I doubt not, yet to me
One line than none would better be.

But tell me now about yourselves.
  Have bride and bridegroom come?
And are you severing the chain
  That binds you to your home?
And will the first of April find
You busier still with hand and mind?

Planning the social sitting-room,
  The chamber for the guest.
The husband prompt, as husband should,
  To do his wife's behest,
And taxing ingenuity
To make the haven meet for thee.

'Twill never be as that dear home
  From which your feet are straying;
There parents' voices have been heard,
  There children have been playing.
There have they grown beneath your eye;
There have you parted company.

There death has entered, but a smile
  Greeted the spoiler as he came;
While kindly, solemnly, he placed
  His hand upon the flickering flame.
And gray heads bowed in fervent prayer,
'Twas silence all—they were not there.

During the first year of our residence on the Woodland farm, our son, Edward M. Paxson, married Mary Caroline Newlin, daughter of Nathaniel and Rachel Newlin.

Our three sons had now all made their selections of a companion for life, and the fact was thus commemorated in verse:

THE THREE BRIDES.

ADDRESSED TO A DAUGHTER-IN-LAW.

I saw thee, fair and lovely one,
  Upon thy bridal day;
When pleased I gave my first-born son
  To own thy gentle sway.

17

Thy look of blended bliss and care,
  I see it—even now;
The orange blossom in thy hair,
  Thy calm and noble brow.

But not with gliding years could flee
  One charm of mind or face,
They only changed thy girlish glee
  To quiet matron grace.

Another, loved from childhood's hour
  For truthful, artless charms,
Came as a cherished favorite flower
  To fond maternal arms.

True feeling lights her dove-like eye,
  A ray so pure and meek;
We almost passed unheeded by
  The rose that tints her cheek.

But virtues that survive the reign
  Of beauty's transient power,
With holier spell will yet remain
  To cheer life's evening hour.

A third sweet daughter comes to bless
  My happy home and heart;
To meet a mother's fond caress,
  And finished joys impart.

With mingled dignity and ease,
    An eye of changeful hue,
We almost fancy we can trace
    The bright thoughts glancing through.

I see her cheek of roseate bloom,
    Her form of seraph grace;
And mark the playful smile illume
    Her music-breathing face.

And prouder, happier far my lot
    To call these treasures mine,
Than all the gems that wealth e'er bought
    On regal brows to shine.

I will introduce here another letter of my sister's, partly on account of the allusion to my sons, which I consider very discriminating, and still more because it unfolds traits of her character that appear nowhere else on these pages:

FOURTH MONTH, 1854.

I write now, dear sister, because I know thee will expect a letter by this post, though without much qualification for the task, yet I am better than for the last few months, and perhaps I ought not to expect better health in my sixty-fourth year,* and am favored to feel resigned

---

* She had eleven years previous an impression this would be her last.

to what is apportioned me; the lameness in my shoulder is considered incurable.

We miss our neighbors even more than I expected; no bright glances come from the now closed shutters, which no fair hand opens, as in the happy past. I felt when we parted that we could not meet as we had met, and felt it too deeply to rhyme about it; indeed, my nerves were disturbed so much by the idea that I could not write neatly, as I wished, the little Valedictory I sent her.

Thee once observed that I was always interesting when she was the theme, and if it was so it is easily accounted for. The thousand devices, often ingenious and amusing, and always friendly and obliging, were a great stimulus to the intellect. Beside, I always enjoyed the neighborhood tie, and this was in perfection. Churchmans', of German-town, in a somewhat different way, were equally agreeable as neighbors, but Rebecca Earl's youth and beauty seemed to give a fairy-like charm, which her playfulness enhanced.

To her the following lines, from a poem entitled "My Neighbor," fully apply :

> "To spread the mental feast is thine,
> The sage's thought, the poet's line,
> If thou possess them they are mine,
> My Neighbor."

How I do love these visits without preparation, this continual interchange of courtesies; "the household news so earnestly related, and small domestic cares," have a perpetual charm for me.

I have got to prosing so that I fear I shall have a lack of room to say all I intended; but I must tell thee how much we were pleased with S. J. Paxson's visit made us last week; his uncle said he never liked him so well before, and I was charmed with his frankness in at once making himself at home; he installed himself in the proffered rocking-chair without ceremony, and I felt, in his manner and the tones of his voice, that he was no stranger, but my own dear sister's son, whom I had so often held in my arms in the olden time. I always felt a deep interest in him, seldom as I have seen him lately, from hearing so much of his warm-heartedness from thee.

Albert I have seen more of from the circumstance of his remaining longer under the parental roof than his brothers; he always reminds me of some lines, written by I know not whom, but I consider them very applicable to him:

"The happy, grateful spirit that improves
  And brightens every gift by fortune given;
  That wander where it will with those it loves,
  Makes every place a home, and home a heaven."

With Edward, "the youngest of dear ones that sat on thy knee," I have had less personal intercourse than with either of the others, yet do I feel not less acquainted with him. I used to welcome with pride as well as pleasure the *Newtown Journal* to our home, when he was its editor; of my appreciation of his editorials and other essays, my valued scrap-book bears ample witness.

E. P.

Not far from the date of the above letter, I made the acquaintance of Sarah G. Rich, of Philadelphia, who had a large circle of admiring and sympathizing friends. She was confined to her bed thirteen years, unable even to change her position without assistance; yet she had many correspondents, for she retained the use of her hands and wrote lying on her back, with her head slightly elevated, and had a small desk placed on her breast. She was a remarkable instance of cheerfulness and resignation through suffering, often intense as well as protracted, and her patience seemed unfailing.

I corresponded with her for the last few years of her life, and of the large number of her letters in my possession, I will at least copy one as a memorial of her.

I have lately seen, with pleasure, several of her letters published in *Friends' Intelligencer*.

LETTER FROM S. G. RICH. 1854.

The impression is on my mind to write to thee, my dear friend; and very often before have thoughts arisen that, had we been side by side, I should have expressed to thee; but on taking the pen, such a dearth seemed to possess me that, if I did not feel that the present moment only is ours, and in my case emphatically so, I should be induced to lay it aside, and only commune with thee in spirit without invoking the aid of words to assure thee of my heart's treasured love.

More than usual suffering has been my portion for many weeks past, and of a nature to disqualify me for enjoying my many blessings, and also to convince me that disease is doing its work, though a long time may be requisite to consummate the whole design of this life.

On the other hand, I feel that in wisdom it may be that all in a brief space may be brought to a close; all that I ask, in either view of the case, is strength and patience to hold out to the end; be it long or short, it matters not, if only sustained by that Power who is ever ready, if called upon, to arise and hold in subjection the winds and waves that the tossed mind has believed must swallow it up.

Oh, what beauty and safety there is in a childlike confidence in that Arm which, though unseen, is with us still! This is the increasing desire of my heart; then could I, in truth, make Longfellow's words my own: "Look not mournfully into the past, it returns not again; wisely improve the present, it is thine. Go forth into the shadowy future without fear, and with a manly heart."

I have received two letters from thee since I wrote, and assure thee I am truly a grateful receiver of thy many favors evincing so deep an interest in thy suffering friend, and I may say, in sincerity, that a true appreciation of such love and interest is one of the sweetest solaces of my life, for what would life be to me without such sympathy? My joys are narrowed down to converse with the few, comparatively speaking, who seek the seclusion of a sick-chamber to bestow that friendship which is as the oil of gladness to the heart of the sufferer.

It is a balm not to be surpassed, except that bestowed by the Physician of souls; but every act of sympathy and love is an emanation from the source of love itself, hence the invigorating influence upon the heart of the grateful recipient.

Thy letter received yesterday was very welcome indeed, for I could well understand that it must be a sacrifice to leave intellectual company to write a diary for me; this gave it additional value.

I was in mind tracing you along day by day, hoping you would meet with my dear Rachel Sharpless on your Chester County journey; she is one who possesses "greenness in old age," and the society of such as she is as refreshing as a brook by the wayside to the weary traveller. By example holding up the language, "Follow us, as we have followed Christ."

We are lonely here now, so many of the family are out of town; but J. Gillingham Fell is at home, and a host in himself, for he embodies so much that makes every one comfortable around him.

Oh, dear Nancy! what dependent creatures we are upon one another, and this we do not realize till likely to have some one wrested from us on whom we have been wont to lean. The truth of this reflection my situation for the last twelve years deeply impresses on me.

But Christ is my salvation, what shall I fear? Oh! that my faith may more and more increase, trusting that as goodness and mercy have followed me all· the days of my life, such will in matchless mercy be continued to me, till in His unerring wisdom He shall be pleased to say, " Now let Thy servant depart in peace !"

S. G. R.

There appears to be a vast difference in the opinion of mankind as to which is the happiest period of human life, and the point will probably remain unsettled, as there is no certain criterion by which to judge it. The poets, who have, though we may not be aware of it, more influence in forming our opinions than almost any class of the community, disagree on this subject. One of them exclaims,—

" Give me back, give me back the wild freshness of morning!
Her clouds and her tears are worth evening's best light."

Another, and perhaps more reliable one, tells us that
" Age has pleasures of its own
That age can only know."

18

In what those enjoyments consist he does not inform us, nor would it be easy to define them, as so much depends on the natural temperament; one thing, however, aged persons have in common,—they can all look back upon a long course of years, which, if they have been spent in a manner manifesting love to God and love to man, will be a continual theme for agreeable reflections.

There is evidently a great disparity in our outward situation while on earth, but whether there is an equal degree in the amount of happiness I am doubtful.

Some dispositions seem by nature formed for bliss, and such as these will be likely to have a share of it through all the various trials of life; while others are surrounded by all that renders life desirable, and neglect to secure the happiness that seems to us within their reach.

As regards myself, I am glad to believe that the first-mentioned order of mind predominates in my temperament.

In a late letter from my friend, Phebe Ann Wright, is the following sentence, which does not seem irrelevant to the subject before us:

. . . Altogether, it seems to me, many of the good things of this world have befallen you. Some of them are doubtless the result of the lives you have lived, but sometimes meritorious persons are very unfortunate; yet most persons, perhaps, give a shape to the circumstances that surround them.

One of the enjoyments of age I possess in an eminent degree. I love to look back upon early friendships, even those formed in childhood; and those that did not survive that period are still remembered with pleasure, for they were always soon succeeded by others, and the void they left was not long perceptible.

Some intimacies, however, thus early formed lasted till life's decline, and will still occupy a place in its cherished memories. Among the most conspicuous on this list was Julia Carey. She was near my own age, and one of those that attended the school in my father's house.

With the avidity that girls of thirteen contract friendships ours was formed, and cemented by congeniality of pursuits and tastes. After our school-days were over the friendly intercourse was still continued, and I was her bridesmaid when she was married to Dr. C. D. Hampton.

They settled for a time in Cincinnati, where he was a successful practitioner of medicine. While they resided there her husband met occasionally with the inhabitants of Union Village, a Shaker settlement, thirty miles from their home; they made him a convert to their faith, and he soon after settled among them as their physician.

Julia at first felt considerable reluctance to the measure, but became at length quite satisfied with her home; and they appeared to appreciate her character, for they soon appointed her Lady Abbess, or, as they termed the office, " Spiritual Deaconness," and she had power and influence among them.

She no doubt rendered them essential service, for she was the means of establishing among them a large library of well-selected books,—she found none there, except a few volumes relative to their peculiar tenets; but she had before her death the satisfaction of seeing many cultivated persons around her, and the pleasure of knowing that her energetic exertions had mainly produced the change.

She had a mind above the common order, was attractive in her appearance, and her ma ners were gentle and refined. In connection with this, I remember some lines written by one who had been her school-mate, on hearing she had united herself to that sect:

Though strange to us it seemeth
The lot she chose to share;
Light from her pathway beameth,
She walks an angel there.

Before I speak of our latter days of intimacy, I will copy the first letter I had from her after her change of faith; it gives a clear and pretty full account of her feelings with respect to it, but does not allude at all to the conspicuous position she maintained in that establishment then, and continued to hold till called upon to "give up her stewardship."

UNION VILLAGE, OHIO, 1851.

MY DEAR FRIEND,—I feel the truest pleasure in acknowledging the receipt of the little volume thou wast kind enough to send me, and return my sincere thanks. It is a precious gem in my estimation, and, as might be expected, brought with it many agreeable associations connected with my youthful days, and at the same time convinced me that I still hold a place in thy memory in defiance of an absence of more than thirty-five years.

I have never forgotten the kind treatment I received while a resident in thy father's family, neither has my attachment to each member of it in the least abated; but it is a pleasant spot in memory, where my mind often lingers with delight. We were happy, innocent children, were we not?

I well remember the sorrow I experienced at parting with friends I had learned to love so dearly. No doubt a change has come over the face of the landscape, and many of its inhabitants have been removed by death; yet when I cast a glance back at the scenes of my childhood and youth, I still have a very clear view of things as they were: the garden, the orchard, the school-room, and even the old majestic mulberry-tree before thy father's door, and my own native spot of earth are as vivid in my memory as if I had seen them but yesterday.

Although I often look back to the blessings enjoyed in early life, I have no cause to complain of the dealing of Providence with me since coming to riper years. Our lot has been cast in a beautiful and fertile land, abounding in all the necessaries and luxuries of life, and is thought to be as rapidly improving as any part of the Union.

You have doubtless heard something of our manner of living, and of the "people, strange and rude," with whom we reside; but thou, my dear friend, hast lived long enough and experienced sufficient to know that mere report is not always to be relied on. The truth is that visitors who come among us with prejudiced minds often form mistaken notions concerning us, and report accordingly, and this accounts in some measure for the unfavorable things that have been circulated against us. We have, it is true, renounced our former manner of living, and for no other reason but that we might live a life of purity and holiness, and thereby fit our souls for heavenly enjoyments. We believe, as did thy own dear mother, that the enjoyments of the spirit world bear no resemblance to the gratifications of sense; but be assured, my dear friend, that the sacrifice we are called to make does not lessen our enjoyments, but, on the contrary, greatly enhances them.

The reflection that we are living that life that accords with the precepts and example of our blessed Saviour, and of course is well pleasing to our Heavenly Father, is amply sufficient at all times to reward us for relinquishing the perishing enjoyments of time. I will now tell thee about our manner of living, but it will be but a faint outline, as I shall not have room for more.

We hold a joint interest, and live in large families; ours numbers one hundred and sixty, male and female; we live together and enjoy each other's society as good brethren and sisters. Rich and poor all come on a level, and temporal provision is made for all that require it. If any are sick, we have a building set apart for their accommodation, where the physician and nurses give them all the attention necessary for their comfort.

How is our dearly loved Eliza Pickering, one of the ever cherished friends of the olden time, and probably separated from me till our earthly pilgrimage is ended? But we know not what an entrance into the spirit world may introduce us to, and that cannot be at an immense distance from any of our age.

If I have been sadly in arrears before, I think thou wilt be willing to cancel the debt by the time thee comes to the end of this letter; and now I must say farewell, in that love will never know change or decline.

JULIA C. HAMPTON.

Ever after the reception of the foregoing letter we corresponded steadily till her death, which took place in her seventy-sixth year. They took with them to Union Village a son and daughter, who still remain there.

There was something rather remarkable in the termination of our correspondence, of which I will give here a very brief sketch.

We dreamed of each other the same night, and each next morning embodied the dream in a letter to the other. These letters were on their way at the same time.

She says,—

I dreamed last night of having a letter from thee. The envelope seemed very full, and I thought what a treat I shall have; but alas, I was doomed to disappointment, for I could not even find the right page to begin on. May the first but not the latter part of my dream be realized.

My son and I have both written to thee within a few

months. If writing did not tax my energies more than anything else, thee would hear from me oftener.

Of my letter, bearing the same date as hers, I will also give an extract:

Seldom have I been in arrears to thee so long. I often intended to write on the morrow, but to-morrow has always been noted for deceiving.

Perhaps this state of affairs might have continued still longer had I not, last night, had a dream of thee that forcibly impressed my mind.

I had, through this medium, a visit from thee, exactly as thee appeared in thy early womanhood, smiling on me as in former days,—the same tones, low and sweet, that used to greet my ear in the still remembered olden time. Thee spoke of our childhood's pastimes in my father's orchard, our visits to Lahaska Mountain to gather flowers to deck our rustic arbor. In short, many past scenes of pleasure were brought into view; but the delight with which thee dwelt on them did not find in my bosom an answering tone, for I felt sensibly the disparity of years, and that we were less companionable to each other than in early days, seemed the prevailing idea in my mind.

After a short visit, thee wrapped thy mantle around thee and glided away with almost unearthly grace; but thee said no farewell word, yet I will not imitate thee in this particular, but bid thee a fond farewell.

"May seraphs smile and mortals weep
When angel hands have crowned thee."

19

Little more than a week after the letters passed between us from which I have made these extracts, I received one from her son. The letter was long and very interesting. I will copy a part of it, which must be read with interest, as taken in connection with the previous account:

TO A. J. PAXSON.

DEAR FRIEND,—Your kind letter to our gentle and affectionate mother reached us the very day of her departure to a better world, but too late for her loving eyes. She wrote to you a day or two before her death. Truly may it be said, your friendship claimed some of her latest thoughts, even on to the very brink of Jordan.

I would gladly, if I could, say something to console you on this our mutual bereavement; but we have, I trust, realized, and I doubt not it is also your experience, that "There is healing balm in Gilead, and a Physician there," who is able to console us, even for the loss of life-long friends.

Time, the great healer of all grief, will no doubt allure us in his gradual manner from our tender regrets, and slowly heal the wounds he has inflicted through his dread Prime Minister.

Farewell. May Heaven lead, comfort, and bless you every moment of life, is the sincere prayer of your friend,

OLIVER C. HAMPTON.

In the third summer of our residence at Woodlawn Farm, Thomas took a journey to the West, in company with his sister, Jane Price, and Elizabeth Peart, both public Friends, whose mission was a religious visit to the society in that part of the vineyard. During the four months of their absence from home they attended the Yearly Meetings of Ohio and Indiana, and many subordinate ones, besides making social visits to many of their friends. They spent a few days with John and Anna P. Cooper, and found them pleasantly situated.

During the fifth summer of their wedded life, Albert lost his affectionate and beloved companion. For more than a year she had discovered symptoms of that dreaded disease which has so often for its victims the young and lovely. She was perfectly resigned to her early departure, and a pattern of patience through her sickness.

A few weeks previous to her death she asked me to read to her Mrs. Sigourney's lines on leaving "A Rural Residence," and she repeated after me, with much emphasis and feeling, the following lines, that seemed to me descriptive of her own state of mind:

"Praise to our Father—God,
  High praise in solemn lay;
Alike for what His hand has given
  And what it takes away."

The evening after her funeral I endeavored to embody in a short poem some of the memorable expressions she uttered the last week of her life. Though they may be imperfect as poetry, they give a faithful view of her converse at that period:

PARTING WORDS.

He comes for me, an angel form,
  That guides the spirit from the clay;
And to my soul a life-glow warm
  Reveals, as from celestial day.

He comes a holy, welcome guest.
  No shadows dim his plumage fair;
He points me to my Heavenly rest,
  And shows the glories beaming there.

He comes—my Albert, soon we part,
  And thou, dear, prattling babe, farewell;
How dear to this fond, faithful heart
  Only an angel's tongue could tell.

But not the pure and sacred joys
  That crowned my peaceful Eden home,
Could lure me from the Heavenly voice
  That calls to raptures yet to come.

Though shrouded in the silent tomb,
  No vernal morn may meet my sight;
For me a fadeless spring shall bloom,
  That knows no wasting winter blight.

I see cherubic robes of light
  Unfold to my enraptured gaze,—
Too weak to bear the glorious sight
  Or join the ecstatic songs of praise.

An Arm Divine is round me now;
  My fainting soul grows clear and strong;
" 'Tis finished"—at His word I bow,
  And haste to join the angelic throng.

Albert not inclining to remain at Walnut Grove after the death of his wife, we sold the property, and he and his daughter, Mary, came to reside with us, where he remained a year, and then went to live with his brother, S. J. Paxson, at Doylestown, leaving Mary under our care.

In 1854 he married Lavinia S. Ely and settled at her paternal home, she being now the only living child of her parents.

In the spring of 1856, having relinquished housekeeping, we commenced boarding with William and Roseanna Morris. Her family name was Scott. She was a near relative of

General Winfield Scott. Debbie Ann, their only child, whom I named myself during my first acquaintance with her mother, added much to the happiness of Mary's childhood; they were nearly of an age, and constant playmates and companions.

On my own part, I felt it quite a relief to lay down the burden of housekeeping, yet still retain my accustomed home, in which I could receive my friends with all the freedom and hospitality of former days.

I had been in the habit of telling my friends that I did not expect to be always fettered by worldly cares, but meant to indulge myself in life's decline in reading, writing, or any congenial pursuit that inclination prompted. We many years before had talked of giving up domestic care for one year, that we might visit our distant friends without feeling that any duty was neglected by so doing. But we eventually concluded if we threw off our trammels for a brief space, we might not be willing to resume them; therefore adopted the thorough emancipation principle..

I fear that my naturally sanguine temperament had led me to hope too much, and endeavored to keep in mind the ten days of Seged, Lord of Ethiopia; but I can say with gratitude that my early expectations and reveries on this subject have been more than realized.

When the fact of our liberation from care became known among our friends, we had many invitations to visit them. Phebe Ann Wright, of Wilkesbarre, in one of her letters, says, "I congratulate thee on the new arrangement you have made, though I always thought Thomas and thyself had the faculty of disposing of the cares of life in the smoothest possible way. Now you no longer need the gift, just transfer it to me, at least for a season, and bring it with thee when thee makes thy visit."

But though more at liberty, that circumstance did not cause us to visit extensively; we have almost ever since we were boarders made a few weeks' visit to our brothers and sisters in Chester County, as well as other relatives in that place, but that has been the extent of our journeyings.

We generally attended Concord and Caln Quarterly Meetings. Oliver and his wife, Jane, lived there several years, and we often met many agreeable friends at their house. They removed before his death to the neighborhood of West Chester, where most of my husband's near relatives are located, and we have enjoyed our summer excursions there exceedingly.

Brother Jacob and his wife, Maria, by settling there, has added much to the attraction the place had before in our eyes.

I have also been accustomed to spend a few weeks in Philadelphia during the autumn of each year, but that I have not recently done. The last visit I remember with peculiar pleasure; I may probably never repeat it, but the recollection will always be a pleasant one, for even in my youthful days I never made one that I enjoyed more, or that the retrospect afforded more unmingled satisfaction.

I of course made many visits, but a day spent with Hannah Howell and her sister, Rachel H. Newlin, was especially delightful. The former is not far from my age, and we had in early life so many of the same acquaintance, that on this occasion our fund of conversation was almost inexhaustible.

Her sister is younger; but we, too, had many of the same intimate friends of both sexes, and, above all other considerations, she is the mother of my beloved daughter, Mary C., and that is of itself a strong tie.

I also met at her mother's residence Rachel Walton, from New Brighton, of whom I had lately seen but little; she was looking as well as when I attended her wedding in that very same house several years before. Time seemed to have left on her few of his distinctive marks. She was spending a month with her aged mother and two sisters, long since on my list of true and faithful friends.

I also spent a day with my friend and correspondent, Ann Preston. She took me to see the Woman's Medical College, and I was much interested in every detail of hers respecting it. We also visited the Woman's Hospital connected with the first-named institution. She is the medical attendant, and I accompanied her through all the wards to see the invalids, about twenty in number. The gratitude that some of them evinced by their manners, as well as expressions, showed plainly their appreciation of the kindness and tenderness that sought to cheer and alleviate their sufferings.

In the fall of 1847 our sister, Jane Price, felt an impression of duty to visit the families of Buckingham Monthly Meeting, and came on that mission among us, accompanied by her husband, Benjamin Price. We were appointed by our meeting as companions for them on the service. I was prevented by indisposition most of the time, but was with them one week, much to my satisfaction.

Many interesting incidents occurred during that time, one of which I will narrate, as it has since been oftener in my mind, perhaps, than any other.

At a house where we stopped, expecting to make a little visit, as was our custom, we found the family consisted of only a man and his wife, the former from home. The wife received us very kindly, but informed us that though her husband was a member of our society she was not. Thomas then observed, " Perhaps, as that is the case, thee would not care about our making the visit here that we had contemplated." She replied so earnestly that we could not doubt her sincerity, "Indeed I would;" and, as she had no fire in sitting-room or parlor, and the morning was cool, she invited us into her kitchen, where we found a comfortable fire.

We sat down with her, quite satisfied with our location, and she seemed too much pleased to have our company to think much about the place of reception. As soon as perfect quiet reigned, my mind became occupied with these lines of Whittier:

"Where are the sisters who hastened to greet
The lowly Redeemer and sit at his feet?"

I suppose there was something in her manner that reminded me of them; I had never met her before, and to me her deportment was striking.

Humility and a kind of subdued sadness marked her appearance; we found in a subsequent conversation with her that she had just buried two children.

While I was dwelling on the lines above mentioned, sister Jane gave me a searching glance that I did not comprehend at the time, but was afterward explained. The first thing Jane said was to repeat the passage of Scripture that these lines refer to, and made interesting comments thereupon. I had felt quite an inclination to speak them aloud, but it seemed to be an interference with Jane's privilege; and had I done so, might always have supposed I had pointed her mind in that direction.

I asked her, after we left the house, why she gave me that earnest look; she replied, "Because I knew thee withheld something." I then told her the facts of the case, observing that as it happened, no one was a loser; she responded, "No one perhaps but thyself, for I believe thee did not attend to the requirements of duty in the case;" and she may have been correct.

About the year 1858 an article appeared in our Bucks County newspaper, extracted from the works of Bancroft, the historian, respecting the writings and character of Dr. Johnson. I considered it an unfair and incorrect statement, and was thereby induced to write an essay for the *Intelligencer* on the subject. Not that I for a moment supposed that anything from my pen was needed, but merely for the relief of my own mind.

I have since been glad that I yielded to the impulse to do so, for it was the means of bringing about an acquaintance with Samuel Austin Allibone, which probably but for that circumstance would not have taken place. He was then preparing for the press his "Biographical Dictionary of English Literature," a work requiring immense perseverance and research, and by which he has laid the reading community under great obligations, and justly won the title of "The Immortalizer of Authors."

DR. SAMUEL JOHNSON.

MESSRS. EDITORS:

I observed in a late number of the *Intelligencer* an article from the pen of Bancroft, the historian, respecting which I desire to make a few remarks.

The article in question is an unscrupulous attack on the character and genius of Dr. Johnson, and calculated to excite profound surprise, as a motive is evidently wanting for such an extraordinary perversion of facts. In every point of view such want of accuracy is to be deplored, for when we find a historian forsaking the path of integrity and truth in one instance, we naturally lose our confidence in his whole narrative. The great luminary alluded to ought not to be a stranger to the literary world, as his biography has been presented to the public four times at

least, written, too, both by friend and foe, with the utmost
minuteness; and among them all, we feel that we know him
almost as well as though he had in life walked in our
midst.

The first and only well-founded charge brought against
him is his poverty. He was, it is true, obliged for several
years to provide for the day that was passing over him;
but I suspect he would not, later in life at least, be willing to repine at a cause that contributed to so mag-
nificent an effect, even the formation of a name that will
only be forgotten when the English language sinks into
oblivion.

This candid reviewer of character notices his generosity
to the needy, but in a manner so ambiguous that his
readers are doubtful whether he intends it for eulogy or
censure.

He did certainly shelter in his hospitable domicile several
indigent persons, and his discrimination was as conspicuous
as his charity, for of those who shared his benevolence was
the blind poetess, Miss Williams, whose father had in early
life bestowed on Johnson some kindness, and his grateful
heart prompted this liberal return. Dr. Levett also shared
his home for years,—his only claim thereto was poverty and
merit.

The pension granted him by Government, respecting
which Bancroft has made such injurious remarks, representing it as a political bribe, his biographer refutes from
the most authentic information. It was granted solely as
a reward of his literary labors. Lord Bute, when he noti-

fied Dr. Johnson of it, made this explicit declaration, " It is not given you for anything you are to do, but for what you have done."

And no marvel is it that his native country should delight to honor and to benefit an author whose writings she had adopted as standard works; whose pen had diffused her literary fame over the civilized world, for they have been translated into most of the modern languages, and will through all time maintain their just place in minds capable of appreciating their excellence and beauty.

His dictionary, the labor of years, was a strong claim on the liberality of the Government. The French nation, about the same period, appointed forty learned men for the same service, and they were longer in performing the task than Johnson's unaided pen.

Bancroft has discovered that he is not a man of genius. On this point we must award him the credit of originality, as it is probably the first time such an idea suggested itself to any rational mind. Nor will we refute the charge, except by pointing to the Rambler, to "Rasselas." But it is difficult to know when to desist when we would enumerate the beauties of Johnson. "Rasselas" was written in the evenings of one week, and a more delightful composition does not grace a language.

As a poet, too, he stands pre-eminent. The "Vanity of Human Wishes" is considered as high an effort of ethic poetry as has appeared in any language. Such was the opinion of Sir Walter Scott, of Lord Byron, and a host of others who stand high in the rolls of literary fame.

His physical temperament was unpropitious to the perfect enjoyment of life, and to this circumstance may reasonably be ascribed that morbid state of mind that sometimes appeared in after-years.

He lived, however, to a good old age, and died, says his biographer, "full of resignation, strengthened in faith and joyful in hope."

How different from the dark picture drawn by his calumniator!

LETTER FROM S. AUSTIN ALLIBONE.

1863.

MY DEAR MRS. PAXSON,—My cousin Mary, your daughter, promised me that I should have the pleasure of seeing you, and last Saturday evening was fixed on for that purpose. Let me express the hope that the indisposition which hastened your departure has been succeeded by entire restoration to health.

I was not a little pleased to hear of the good opinion which you expressed of my biographical labors, so far as they are embodied in the first volume of my " Dictionary of English Literature." It is a great satisfaction to be assured of the cordial approval of those whose literary pursuits in the same department of research gives great value to their verdict.

I anticipate with pleasure your perusal of volume second (and last), on which I have been for some years, and still am very busily engaged, as it contains, by alphabetical necessity, more names of interest than are to be found in volume first, for instance, Lamb, Macaulay, Milman, Mackenzie, More (Sir Thomas, the great), Moore (Thomas, the little), Motley, Reid, Scott, Shakespeare, Thomson, Tennyson, Warburton, Pope, Swift, and a thousand others.

I am gratified that you especially commend my life of Dr. Johnson, whom we both so greatly admire, and I beg you to accept my thanks for your well-written dressing of Mr. Historian Bancroft. It reminds me of Mrs. Knowles' castigation of the great Johnson, only that the comparison by no means holds good of Bancroft.

If you will send me a copy of that piece I will send it to Bancroft, with a letter, and we will see what he can say for himself.

Allow me to congratulate you upon the great and deserved success of your son, Edward, one of my most highly-valued friends. He has already risen high, and is rapidly rising higher; is in great honor and reputation with the Bar and (I doubt not) the Bench.

Begging you to let me know when you will again be in the city, that we may have some converse respecting the Giants of olden time, I am, madam, with great respect, your friend,

S. AUSTIN ALLIBONE.

In 1863 I had a visit from Frances D. Gage. I had long wished to meet with her, but it was an event that I rather wished than expected, as our homes were remote from each other.

21

Though not a native of Ohio, she was at that time a resident there, and had come on to deliver lectures on various subjects. They were well attended, and the proceeds thereof devoted to the aid of the sufferers from the disastrous war that had desolated so many of the once happy homes of our country.

I was not able to attend her lectures, being confined most of that winter to my chamber with neuralgia in my head, which affected my eyes so much that I was obliged partially to exclude the light for some months.

I should have enjoyed her visit at any time, and almost under any circumstances, but it was especially soothing to my feelings as I was then situated.

My previous knowledge of her was obtained only through her writings. Occasionally very interesting tales from her pen met my eye, but principally from her poetry I felt the interest of a personal friend.

Washington Irving says, "The intercourse between the poet and his readers is ever new, active, and immediate," and I realized it in the present instance.

My first knowledge of her, except through this medium, was a letter from my friend, Ann C. Levis, who alluded in it to Frances D. Gage. It was many years previous to her visit among us; as I consider the letter very interesting, I will make here an extract from it:

Since I last wrote I attended a convention at West Chester, on the subject of "Women's Rights," and was much interested, as there were several able speakers present, and many letters read from those that were prevented attending. I would gladly tell thee much that passed, but my memory is so frail that I often only retain the shell and lose the substance.

I remember a remark by a lady of Vermont, that poor mother Eve ate the apple which we are informed was the knowledge of good and evil, and turned the world upside down. Frances D. Gage, of Ohio, perhaps not the most eloquent speaker, but more talented as a writer, replied, that she hoped the women of the present day would eat another, and turn it back again.

It was a treat, I assure thee, to hear a discussion from such gifted women. But while on this subject I must tell thee of Elizabeth Oaks Smith's late visit to West Chester. She delivered there a lecture on this subject, which I did not hear, but learned she made converts even among those most opposed to her views. She is among our ablest writers, and some of her similes are beautiful; of such is the following:

"The dew of the mountain even tires of its isolation, and mounts upward to the sky, where it rejoices in the rainbow.

"The seed struggles mightily in the dark earth, for the green leaf and beautiful blossom lie folded within, calling for light.

"The worm sickens at the dust of its dim way, for the wings of the butterfly call for a higher life.

"Everywhere the voices of God from within cry, 'Where art thou?' and yet we hide ourselves, and find excuses for our inaction."   A. C. LEVIS.

Frances D. Gage remained with us but one night and part of the next day, as her engagements prevented a longer visit. Before she left us she wrote a little poem and left it in her room, and it solaced the lonely hours after her departure.

Though completely an impromptu, we recognize in it the poetess, whose muse has interested us so often and so long.

TO MRS. A. J. PAXSON.

Little recked I long ago,
  When thy pleasant thoughts I read,
That I e'er should live to know
  One so loved when years had sped.

That the pleasure should be mine
　Thy kind voice of love to hear,
Speaking cheerful words of thine
　For my ready listening ear.

Mother!—may I call thee so?—
　Thou a lesson good hath taught,
One that every soul should know,
　Of great strength and wisdom fraught.

That the soul may yet be young,
　While the years, threescore and ten,
Mar the body and the tongue,
　Give back youth and joy again.

Ne'er shall I forget this day,
　Bright amid its cloud and storm;
It will cheer me on the way,
　Nestling in my heart to warm.

Daily as I wander on
　Blessings rich around me fall;
Father! thanks for this last one,
　Richest, dearest of them all.

F. D. GAGE.

It was many years ago, walking in a graveyard
with a friend of mine, who had asked me to
accompany her to the last resting-place of her

nine children. I told her, and she seemed to consider it a remarkable fact, as I was then near fifty years of age, that no near ties of kindred had been severed in my case; parents, husband and children, sister and brother, had all yet been spared to me. She observed, "I doubt if any woman of the same age can say the same in this section of the country." I had not taken this view of the subject till she drew my attention to it, but when I did reflect upon it I concluded she was correct, for I could recollect none that were in this respect similarly situated.

Soon after I lost my parents, and the next bereavement was by the decease of my sister in 1855. There was no other death in my immediate branch of the family till 1864, when our eldest son was taken from us, by a pulmonary complaint, in his forty-sixth year. Soon after his death, seven different articles respecting him appeared in our county newspapers; all of them written by persons unconnected with him by consanguinity, and of a different bias in religion and politics, at least some of them.

From a few of these I will make extracts, as

they give a pretty correct view of his character, his position in life, and his calm and peaceful departure:

Died, at his residence in Greenville, Buckingham township, on the 28th day of May, Samuel Johnson Paxson, formerly editor and proprietor of the *Doylestown Democrat*, in the forty-sixth year of his age.

June was wreathing the brow of its first-born day with flowers, and roses redolent with incense,—it was the chosen hour, and most appropriate for Johnson's burial time.

As we thoughtfully reclined, sheltered from sunbeams, beneath the shade of a mammoth chestnut-tree, which, doubtless, for a century past has kept faithful watch and ward over the countless ones who sleep in that grave-ground on Buckingham hill-side, there winds slowly up from yonder valley a hearse with pall emblems, bearing within all that is mortal of Samuel Johnson Paxson. Upward and onward moves the long funeral cortege of weeping relatives and sorrow-stricken friends. Into that olden meeting-house, rich and rare in its remembrance,—its many sunny and sad scenes of both bridal and burials,—within its quaint and quiet walls friends true and devoted bear his lifeless form.

It is a solemn spectacle. On those wan features, where in days gone by dwelt the vigor of his indomitable energy and resolution, gaze in long and lingering look his venerable parents, his widowed wife and fatherless daughters, a broken band of brothers, the playmates of his sunny boyhood, the employees of his printing establishment, who will ever regard and revere him, his friends and foes political.

There follows a silence which blooms into grief. A few brief words from the lips of an honored friend; then the sweet, impressive tones of Sarah T. Betts, speaking earnest words of spiritual consolation; the coffin closes; the mourners move with sad step out to yon open grave: to rest and repose we resign him.

In the even-time of his funeral, we were sitting upon the shaded elm porch of his brother, Albert, having a full view of Paxson's valley embosomed home, just as the setting sun was bidding a golden farewell to the bright spire on his farm buildings; and in the unbidden revery which the scene and occasion called forth, it occurred to us that they are much mistaken who thought him to be practical always, and never poetical, battling with the real to the neglect of the ideal.

Not so. We well remember another June day in the years gone by, when lounging leisurely in his editorial room, the conversation turned upon the love which the Switzer cherished for his mountain home, and, after a moment's reflection, he made use of the following expression, which we wrote down at the time and afterwards published:

"Beautiful is that gentle vale that winds in varied loveliness about the base of Buckingham Mountain. Lahaska, thine is a worship spot for poet and painter,—the Mecca shrine of the enthusiast who sips renewed life and vigor from nature's lips ; and to the lover of the picturesque the Cashmere of America.

"Chide and smile if you will, but these sentiments that come up unbidden from the well-spring of feeling will have utterance ; and, let me tell you, the gleams of the rising day-god are more golden, the skies more blue, the streams more musical, the hour of sunset tinged with a deeper crimson within that valley than any other spot on earth to me."

This, coming without design or effort from the lips of the generally considered cool, matter-of-fact business man, evinced the true heart beating within, where a pure taste nestled lovingly amid the rubbish of realities with which he was continually battling. It opened to us a new leaf in his nature, and increased the admiration in which we had previously enshrined him.

A TRIBUTE FROM ANOTHER PEN.

In the last number of your paper you announced the death of Samuel Johnson Paxson, and gave a brief history of his public and private life. With your permission, I send for publication a few imperfect reflections upon the last few months of his life, more immediately connected with a proper preparation on his part for the important change which would soon dissolve his connection with this world and introduce his spirit to an audience with the Great Searcher of Hearts, who is so particular in the notice of all the doings of His creatures, that "a sparrow falleth not to the ground without His notice." For many months the necessity of a proper preparation to meet his Maker seemed to be impressed on the mind of the deceased. In the secret retirement of his chamber, at times when none but God could be present with him, his attention was turned to the necessity of "setting his house in order," and he sought to banish the world and worldly things as much as possible from his mind.

As his outward man seemed to decay this necessity was felt more forcibly, and he was led to inquire, "What must I do to be saved?" That "Spirit that enlighteneth every man that cometh into the world" was striving with his spirit, leading him to seek forgiveness through the great atoning sacrifice once offered for the sins of the whole world. His mind finally became deeply awakened to the importance of heart religion; he came to contemplate his position, and entered upon the work of repentance with a perseverance that found no abatement until his hopes of acceptance were fully realized, and he washed in that "fountain once opened for sin and uncleanness." He went to his Saviour in the prayer of faith, saying he knew He would not cast him off.

It is seldom that any person is so humble under a sense of sin, and who, as a little child, is willing to be instructed in the great principles of salvation.

There was no spasmodic effort, but a calm and heartfelt effort, to lay hold of the blessed promises of the Holy Scriptures. His mind was fully alive to his situation, and, like wrestling Jacob, he was unwilling to let his Saviour go without the blessing.

As his bodily strength failed his faith and hope grew stronger, and did not leave him till he entered the cold stream of death. At one time, after much suffering and prostration of strength, he roused up and said in an audible voice,—

"I am the Resurrection and the Life."

Just as the lamp of life was flickering and about to expire, after bidding those around him an affectionate farewell, he finally exclaimed, "Oh, Lamb of God, I come, I come!" and the spirit that animated his mortal body took its everlasting flight.

It is a solemn thing to die, even where there is substantial hope of happiness to the departed. How much more solemn and terrible is it to die where there is no such hope, and where the soul enters that dark and dreary region of the future without the lamp of the "wise virgin" to cast even a glimmering light upon that untrodden path! Truly may we exclaim in the language of Holy Writ, "What is a man profited if he gain the whole world and lose his own soul?"

As that large and respectable assemblage of human beings, of varied religious professions, gathered around the mortal remains of the deceased in the ancient building of his fathers, and beheld the holy smile that rested on the face of the departed, in the calm embrace of death, it was pleasant to look upon the solemn countenances of all present.

There can be no doubt that many were led to contemplate the time when they too would be called to pay the "debt of nature," and find a lonely resting place in the narrow house to be finally prepared for all the living.

May all who were present on that solemn occasion be so taught "to number their days that they may apply their hearts unto heavenly wisdom."   W. S.

Our son's estimable widow remains at the pretty residence they had recently built, and mutually planned, in which to spend the remainder of their days.

A few weeks previous to her husband's death, their eldest daughter, Helen M., was married to J. Hart Bye, a distant relative of mine, and known and loved almost from "cradle hours;" they have now settled at Helen's mother's, who was very lonely with only her young daughter, Caroline, for a companion. She is yet a school-girl, and though very companionable for her age, could not be expected to supply to her mother the loss of older friends.

Ere I turn from the subject of our son and his family, I will copy some verses written soon after his death:

> Full many a year has passed away
>   Since first maternal joys I knew,
> And clasped thee to my loving breast
>   With instincts tender, fond, and true.

Beloved one, 'twill be now thy turn
　　To thy blest home to welcome me,
As to our world of joys and cares
　　I once with rapture welcomed thee.

No shade there falls on kindred hearts,
　　No veil will shroud our perfect sight;
When safe within our heavenly rest,
　　No storms our union sweet can blight.

Our gracious Father's will has lent
　　Of years threescore and ten to me,
Then may I hope ere long to dwell
　　In that eternal world with thee.

Oh! couldst thou on the confines linger
　　Of that spirit home divine,
Soaring into bliss no farther
　　Till my spirit meets with thine.

The idea embodied in the last verse was suggested by a dream told by my friend, Anna Richardson, of Middletown, Bucks County. A friend of hers, a man about the meridian of life, and in perfect health, had a singular dream, in which he fancied himself passing to the spirit-world, and while on his way thither, came to a dark and rough water that he was obliged to cross over ere he would reach his destination. While gazing upon it, with feelings almost of despair, he discovered, on close investigation, to his great comfort, stepping-stones all the way that would enable him to go through with safety.

On reaching the desired haven he asked for his mother, who had died many years before. He was told that he could not see her yet, "she had gone too far into bliss." About a week after his dream he was attacked by fever and lived but a short time. During his sickness a female public Friend called to see him, and had by his bedside many consoling words to communicate. Among other encouraging expressions she said, "Thee will find stepping-stones all the way. Jesus prepared them for thee long ago."

He then told her his dream, with the assurance that he had never spoken of it to any other person, and acknowledged that she had strengthened his faith that all would be well with him in that future world which he was soon to enter.

The above reliable incident affords one of the many proofs that instruction is sometimes conveyed to the human mind through the medium of dreams; and have we not, beside, the authority

of Holy Writ for believing that such is the case?
In the book of Job we read that "God speaketh
once, yea, twice, yet man perceiveth it not. In a
dream, in a vision of the night, when deep sleep
falleth upon men, in slumberings upon the bed;
then he openeth the ears of men and sealeth their
instruction."

My own dear father, eleven years before his
death, considered himself informed by a dream
of the time of that coming event. He told us
all the particulars next morning, and wrote an
account of them to several of his correspondents.

When the time specified was about half ex-
pired, he became alarmingly ill from fever.
His physician entertained doubts of his recov-
ery, which he seemed to discover, for he said to
me, "I know the doctor's opinion, but it is not
my own. I believe I shall live eleven years, as
my dream led me to expect."

His anticipations on the subject were, as the
event proved, entirely correct.

I have given the foregoing facts relative to
impressions made on the mind in dreams, and
quoted an inspired writer as additional proof

that through this medium many a lesson of instruction is afforded, which, if attended to, can hardly fail of being a benefit to the recipient.

That impressions are frequently made on the mind during our waking hours cannot admit of a doubt, yet it is often interesting to hear details that illustrate this truth, and an incident, told me several years ago by the principal actor in it, is so entirely of this character that I will give it a place here.

Having been making a visit to our Philadelphia friends, we called at our nephew, John Comly's, to dine, on our way home, and there we unexpectedly met a dinner-party. We knew most of those that composed it, but there was a married couple from Germantown that we had never before met, and the idea was simultaneous with the introduction to them, that we had rarely seen so attractive a pair. They were about the medium height and remarkably handsome. This description applied equally to both; but I did not see much of the husband, as I soon left the parlor, feeling disinclined to form acquaintance with strangers or to converse. I was in a few hours to return to that dear home from which I had been absent some weeks, and my thoughts all took that direction, as I had never been so long separated before from Mary, my little granddaughter.

I seated myself on a sofa in the sitting-room, took up a volume that was new to me, and soon became absorbed by its pleasant contents. I had not been long thus engaged when the stranger lady, introduced to me as Jane A——, came and sat down by me. She commenced conversation by asking my opinion of the doctrine of sympathies and antipathies at first sight, courteously ascribing to the influence of the former feeling her leaving the parlor circle for my society. I told her that from early youth, almost from childhood, I had delighted to study the human countenance, and fancied I had acquired some skill in judging of character by the indications thus given, yet acknowledged occasional disappointments in the case in the course of my life-long journey.

That she had also been sometimes mistaken in her decisions she freely coincided, but considered that her first impressions had oftener been correct than otherwise. She then mentioned an

23

event that had occurred the previous summer when this was strikingly the case.

She was travelling in a steamboat, when there entered, and took a seat immediately in front of her, two fashionable and rather imposing-looking females, who appeared from the resemblance to be sisters. To one of these she felt a dislike so decided that she was disposed to call herself to account for it, believing it wrong, and she feared even unchristian, to indulge such feelings as arose in her mind, in the absence of all proof of delinquency in this stranger.

Their proximity was such that she could not readily avoid hearing their conversation, which subsequently proved of considerable service to her.

After she had left the boat and gone some distance in her carriage, she discovered that she had left behind her a basket full of valuable goods; her husband seemed to regard it as a trivial matter, saying that the steward would no doubt take charge of it. But she exclaimed, as by sudden impulse, "That woman has my basket," and the next moment felt a clear assurance that she would recover it; she told her

husband both of these impressions, and he in-
sisted that they were at variance with each other,
for if the suspected person really was in possession of her basket, her probability of obtaining
it was slight.

He inquired whether she knew the name of
the stranger, but she did not, but had found that
she lived in Burlington, from her conversation
with her companion in the boat. He asked if
she wished to go immediately in quest of her
property, but she declined, saying she was not
yet prepared, but was entirely convinced that
she should regain it, and that the same Power
which had so far enlightened her on the subject
would enable her to carry the affair through to
her complete satisfaction.

Next morning she told her husband that she
was now ready to go in search of her basket.
As they rode on their way she recollected the
conversation she had heard the day before, especially the suspected woman telling her companion of a spell of illness she had experienced
about six months previous, and of the skill of a
certain Dr. H——, who had restored her to health
apparently from the verge of the grave.

To this doctor they of course went immediately, but found him suffering from the effects
of a paralytic attack, which affected his mind considerably. She, however, succeeded in making
him comprehend at last all that was needful in
the case, and he gave the street and number of
her residence. When she reached the house, she
recognized it at once to be the same she had
pointed out to her husband as they passed by
it, saying, "I fully believe my basket is in that
house." The door was opened by a child about
five years old; Jane A—— said to her, "Did
your mamma take charge of a basket.for me
yesterday?" "Mamma brought one home,"
was the reply. An important point gained.
"What name shall I take up-stairs?" asked the
child. "Merely say a friend," was the cautious
reply.

Very soon the mother made her appearance,
looking startled and confused. "You took charge
of a basket of mine yesterday," said the unexpected visitor. Jane A—— saw she was about
to frame a denial and hastened to prevent her
by saying, "Your little daughter told me so."
No denial was then attempted, and she brought

the owner her basket, in which nothing had been disturbed.

When she went out to the carriage in which her husband was seated, he said, "I hope you preached her a sermon since you have turned Quaker." She said "No, not what I term a sermon, though perhaps you may. I looked earnestly in her eyes and said, 'If you took charge of this basket for me, I thank you.'"

I think, however, those few words contained much significance and would not soon be forgotten by the erring woman, and would suppose so singular a detection would arrest her in her criminal career; no doubt this would be the case, if she had not wandered too long and far in her erroneous path to be reclaimed.

I have never since met the stranger that interested me so deeply, but have heard of her from many reliable sources,—fully confirming the favorable opinion I had formed from our transient acquaintance. Rarely have I seen a person who combined so many qualifications to interest,—dignified, cultivated, and refined, yet possessing so much native simplicity of character.

Her liberality was an important feature in her

daily life,—she viewed her wealth as a loan that it was her duty as well as a glorious privilege to repay by dispensing comforts to those around her, and in her neighborhood she was a benefactor, for the indigent and suffering

"At her coming steps were glad."

She belonged to the Presbyterian profession of religion, and had mingled but little with the Society of Friends, though the family in which I met her were of that sect, and also her husband's relatives.

In looking over this autobiography I find that I have not mentioned my cousin, Matthias Hutchinson, of Cayuga, New York.

He is my nearest relative by the maternal side, —the only son of my mother's only brother. Of my grandfather Hutchinson's four grandchildren, three yet remain, my brother, William H. Johnson, this cousin, and myself. We have long corresponded, and I will introduce here some letters that will be read with interest.

KING'S FERRY, 12th mo., 1854.

DEAR COUSIN,—I have a long time omitted to answer thy interesting letter, giving so full an account of the changes that have taken place among our relatives and the location and prospects of the survivors.

S. J. P. and Mary C. Paxson had, in letters I had received from them, stated many particulars of thy sister's sickness and death. Truly this has been an eventful year; disease, especially through the heat and drought, has scattered death and affliction over the land with no sparing hand, bearing very many to the tomb, and speaking in solemn tones to us who remain that we also are born to die.

One consolation is still left us, that those who have passed through these scenes of distress to a place of rest can never experience their repetition.

. I have lost no relations in Cayuga the past year, for I had none to lose, but have witnessed the grief of many others. But, amid all, I am gratified to learn that those of my friends who remain are comfortably situated, and their temporal affairs in a prosperous condition.

I am glad to hear that Cousin W. H. Johnson is your county superintendent; his long and deep interest in education must render the office very interesting to him, and I doubt not he has all the requisite qualifications to fill the station in a manner creditable to himself and advantageously to the community.

Jonathan Pickering I trust will be as comfortable as circumstances will admit of. I can sympathize with him, having passed through a similar trial; I am well aware that the shock is a severe one.

Please accept my thanks for those beautiful lines of

Cousin Eliza's, "The Song of Sixty;" they are the more prized because her last.

M. HUTCHINSON.

Extract from a letter dated Seventh month, 1857 :

. . . Thy last communication speaks of the death of Hannamcel Paxson; her memory must be dear to many, and is especially so to me. But few persons excited in her youthful days a more lively interest than she, for, possessing qualities that almost every one admired, it could not be otherwise. The very sound of her name is pleasant, and connected in my mind with unostentatious beauty, purity, and loveliness, with gentleness and patience, with meekness and cheerfulness, and indeed almost every other virtue. Her departure must have been calm, about to enter into a peaceful rest and dwell with holiness. But we must not mourn her loss too much, but prepare to follow her.

I have 'a perfect recollection of her appearance when I was a boy, and remember thinking the angels must look much like her. Her complexion was as smooth as polished marble, where white and red roses seemed beautifully blended; the lovely expression of her eye and lip, so mild yet so cheerful, her unaffected modesty and winning manners, added much to her beauty.

Those only who knew her in early life can judge whether my remarks are just.

S. J. Paxson is about to relinquish his business in Doylestown ; this may be well, his health might suffer, as Edward's undoubtedly did while editing a paper. I am glad to hear that E. and Mary C. are pleasantly located, and his business prosperous. I feel much interest in their affairs.

Thy cousin,

M. HUTCHINSON.

CAYUGA, NEW YORK.

I have in the early part of this autobiography copied two of my sister's letters, and will insert still another.

Letters between near relatives and intimate friends are perhaps mostly engrossed by details only interesting to the recipient, but I think the one now before me will have more general interest.

EXTRACT OF A LETTER TO A. J. P.

About the books thee kindly offered me, I have the life of Elizabeth Fry, and consider it a most interesting work. Friends' books have in times past done me " most essential service," as Mrs. Child says of Thomson and others of her early reading,—but that was an era that can return no more; therefore many things that interested me then are past also, with all their influences, and are as the manna of yesterday to my mind.

They were excellent in their day, even their controversial theology; great men and true were these our worthy ancestors, lineal, spiritual descendants of the sturdy old prophets and martyrs whose hearts were firm and faith

24

strong. Nobly did they dare and do what would appall their degenerate successors even to think of. Not content with fearful denunciations of the sins of priest and people among nations and colonies, but seeking the very stronghold of religious tyranny and bringing the thunder of their spiritual armory to bear upon the Papal anti-Christ himself,—and that face to face.

And they effected a wonderful reformation, for they were the fountain head of those streams that have since found their way, gradually but surely, through all social organizations, forcibly dammed up here and there, but often bursting through all impediments, with a terrible overflow. Testimonies against war, and a blind adherence to spiritual guides, now no longer strange doctrine, had its origin with them, and it was almost a new creation, so completely had the teachings of the blessed Jesus been shrouded in the night of apostasy of which the Protestants had partially lifted the veil.

I should like to read John Comly exceedingly, for he once in his day ignored all building up the sepulchres of our fathers, with the zeal of a Melancthon, not of a Luther or a Fox. He was not, I suspect, of their ardent temperament naturally. I should like to read his thoughts in after-time, written probably as they arose,—when, like Hannah More, he did not want "to reform the reformation." A man of his quiet turn of mind must have a natural horror of anarchy and confusion that a warmer temperament can hardly comprehend.

In the latter part of thy letter thee alludes to our

own society, and it reminded me of our cousin Caleb B. Matthews's observations to thee on this subject in the days of long ago, if I remember correctly, to this effect:

"The society of which we are members may not increase in numbers as in the days gone by, but ought we to regret this, when there is evidence that their influence has been essentially felt, as many of their testimonies have been indorsed, if not always in a society capacity, yet by individuals of every religious organization, and we may rest satisfied in the belief that

> 'Our lamp is only paling
> In Heaven's advancing day.'"

The incidents that I shall next narrate are of a character principally to interest mothers and grandmothers.

I have mentioned in an earlier part of this autobiography that my son Albert, on the death of his wife, gave me his only child to rear and train, and I may probably dwell awhile on this period of my life,—a happier I have never known. She was four years old when she came to us, and as I had never had a daughter, there was a pleasing novelty blended with the feeling of deep responsibility that must and ought to attend the mind when a child, an heir to immortality, is unreservedly committed to our charge. I acknowledge to some anxiety when I remembered the increase of cares and duties such charge would occasion, but this was speedily lost sight of in her affection and docility.

> For well her early prattle pleased,
> And charmed each care away;
> We saw the priceless gems of mind
> Expanding day by day.

She had for the first six years of her residence with us no companion of her own age, but her fondness for dolls, of which she had a large number, seemed to supply the deficiency, and I possibly found her more companionable to me, and derived more amusement from her society, than if her interests had been more diffused.

My sitting-room daily witnessed dozens of these dolls arrayed in their best attire, being taken to their several meeting-houses (as the sideboard, tables, and desk were termed), for most of the religious societies were represented there, and on the occasion of marriages and deaths, as they appeared subject to these casualties, very appropriate discourses were addressed to them by their care-taker.

In her tenth year we commenced boarding with William and Roseanna Morris, and she then first enjoyed the pleasure of constant companionship, as their daughter, Debbie Ann, was near her own age. Their fondness for their needle, and their dexterity in the use of it, was a trait they had in common, and though at first employed on miniature bonnets and dresses, yet it accustomed them to use it to advantage in after-years, when such skill was of consequence to them.

They had a decided taste for the beautiful in nature, and their Christmas-trees, those joint productions of nature and art, manifested much artistic skill. After rejoicing in this pastime a few successive seasons, they abandoned it, and the idea of a miniature mountain, on one side of the sitting-room, engrossed for a short time this fancy.

They found plenty of materials on Lahaska Mountain. There they spent many an hour, gathering mosses of every variety, evergreens, and " many a mossy stone," which they erected against the side of the room with rare taste and beautiful effect.

Travellers, too (of china), might be seen ascending the hill at different stations, emblematic of our earthly pilgrimage, and reposing, as if to rest from the fatigue of climbing so steep an eminence.

At the base was a moss-covered cottage of their own manufacture, and at the door of it a figure representing an old woman in a very plain garb; one hand is extended as if to welcome the wayfarers, and perchance to encourage them in persevering and surmounting all obstacles that may seem to obstruct their upward journey.

Very many persons called to see this Christmas device, and all pronounced it to greatly surpass the pretty specimens of trees of which that festive season is so prolific.

But the days of childhood, like all other days, are fleeting, and womanhood succeeded them almost before we were conscious of her presence. In her eighteenth year she went as a pupil to Moorestown Boarding-School. The principal of the seminary, Mary L. Lippincott, we had long known and highly respected.

There she remained three years, during which she was healthy and happy, and exceedingly enjoyed her temporary home. She became attached to Mary L. Lippincott, and contracted an intimate friendship with the teachers, which, I trust, will remain a pleasant memory through life.

And yet another friendship was formed while there, which will probably render New Jersey her home for life. She became acquainted with Robert Howell Brown, of Burlington County, in that State, a man whose character is entirely congenial with her own, and they were married at our residence, by Friends' ceremony and the approbation of Buckingham Monthly Meeting, on 7th of Second month, 1867.

TO MARY, ON HER EIGHTEENTH BIRTHDAY.

Ten years and eight have passed away
    Since to our gladdened eyes was given
A tiny, fair-haired, lady babe,
    To us a priceless boon from Heaven.

Ah! little dreamed we in that hour
    So fraught with joy to every heart,
That she, the mother, loved and fair,
    From her new treasure soon must part.

Five years the paths of Walnut Grove,
    Serene, that mother's footsteps trod;
Then left our world of joys and cares
    For the blest Paradise of God.

But not to stranger hands consigned
    Was this young scion of her love.
To Woodlawn's peaceful, rural shades
    Was borne that pure and gentle dove.

And gliding years still find her there,
    By hearts encircled true and warm,
Sharing that calm, domestic bliss
    Which gives to life its dearest charm.

"My friends, to many an hour of mine
    Light wings and sunshine you have lent."

Few lines in the whole compass of poetry are oftener remembered by me than those I have just quoted from the poet that so enchanted my youthful fancy, and I feel in age, as forcibly as ever, their beauty and truth, for not in life's meridian or its early dawn had I a larger circle of friends than now gladden my heart in the winter of life.

Dr. Johnson says, "If we do not keep our friendships in constant repair, we shall be left alone in the evening of life." I always felt the power of this reasoning, and, perhaps, acting upon it has kept up my circle of friends, and it seems necessary, when we reflect to how many casualties earth-born friendships are liable. If we live to old age, a large, and, perhaps, the largest number of our associates

"Have gone on the journey we all must go,"

while others, owing either to removal or alienation, are no longer by our side. Mary Drinker, wife of Thomas P. Cope, of Philadelphia, gives an affecting but true view of this subject in some lines published in the *Evening Fire-Side* many years ago:

Ye friends, long severed from my circling arms;
Some rudely torn by force, some drawn by guile;
Some by false reasoning warp'd, and taught to view
Evil for good, through error's misty glass;
Some gliding off with half-reluctant steps,
But most allured by new pursuits, I greet,
In spirit greet you—have ye then forgot
Those juvenile endearments that were formed
In hearts like mine, to twine around its core
In chains no power but cold neglect can break?
Ye friends, so early loved, I love you still;
Still in remembrance swells the pleasing past,
Still in my breast your loved idea lives,
Like the pale shade of dear, departed joy.

The amiable and gifted writer of the above lines seems to have no great confidence in the constancy and truth of human attachments, and though we accept her version of the matter, founded on, I doubt not, an intimate knowledge of human nature and a long experience of life, we only arrive at the conclusion that we will bind still closer to our hearts those that, through every varying scene, really and truly love us.

As regards myself, I have been most fortunate in meeting with so many that have, in defiance of time and absence, continued to me abiding affection. And though, since age and some of its attendant infirmities have been my experience, I have less interest in mingling in general society, the fondness for epistolary converse has somewhat taken the place of verbal intercourse, and having more than fifty correspondents, interspersed through six States of the Union, I am never at a loss for intellectual enjoyments.

As I have occasionally copied in this life-sketch letters from the large collection in my possession, I shall continue, probably, still to do so, when I am sensible that they will be read with interest.

I now select one from the pen of Frances D.

Gage, partly on account of the poetry at its conclusion :

LAMBERTVILLE, Oct. 22, 1865.

DEAR MRS. PAXSON,—Your very interesting letter and the poem of Miss Preston reached me last evening, and were read with great pleasure, and re-read by myself and daughters this morning in the midst of the glowing sunlight and beauty of this exquisite autumnal day, so like thyself, my dear friend, verging into the winter, yet still fresh, and warm, and genial, and sunny. Ah! if all old age was like thine, how it would brighten and sweeten life !

I thank thee indeed for sending me so often glimpses of that noonday sunlight that seems ever in thy heart. Yes, this is a busy world, and those only can tell how busy who have many domestic cares claiming their attention, and at the same time wish to do all their part towards moving the world forward to the great goal of truth and right. I have lately bought a house, into which I hope to enter the first of April; it is very commodious, and I trust I shall feel more at home in it than I have felt since my residence here.

How blest you are in friends! You have always lived in the same neighborhood, and to be known and loved is surely a great blessing. Here I am a stranger, yet daily, I hope, making friends. Your friend and cousin, Harriet M. Foulke, has not called on me, as I hope she yet may.

Why, my dear friend, do you accuse your muse so harshly? I am sure she threw you a pretty plume, even while you were upbraiding her for desertion, and I read your lines with much pleasure, and my daughter Mary also read them with much delight. I have lately had two invitations to silver weddings, and, as I could not attend, I did my part by sending a rhyme for the occasion. As this is your forty-eighth anniversary I send you a copy, hoping it may express my desire to reward you for the good things you send me.

LOVE'S OLD DREAM.

Oh, love's young dream is a beautiful thing
For artist to paint or poet to sing.
Fresh as the roseate dawn of day,
Odorous as bursting buds in May.
Sweet as the wild birds' amorous song,
Warbled the bright spring leaves among.
Pure as the fountain's gushing glow ;
Free as the river's onward flow.
Blest are the hearts where it finds its rest
In life's early spring-time, doubly blest.

But the love that hath outlived the spring
No artist can sketch, no poet sing.
The love that has battled with cares and tears
Through springs and summers of passing years ;
The love that has lasted five and a score
Of autumns and winters is good for more ;
That hath budded and blossomed and stronger grown
For each added joy and each anguish'd moan,
Changing the hues of its mid-day hours
To the deeper tints of autumnal flowers ;
Glowing in beauty as rich and rare
As the grand old trees in the winter air.

Feeling the frosts of the coming time,
Decking the brow with silvery rhyme,
Yet gathering strength in their hearts of oak
To patiently live till the lightning's stroke,
That alone on earth can the true hearts sever,
To join them again in the Grand Forever.
Oh! love's old dream, dreamed o'er and o'er,
And each time sweeter than before,
Is the truest, purest, holiest thing
That artist can paint or poet sing.

F. D. GAGE.

We were invited on the 12th of Sixth month, 1867, to what Frederika Bremer calls a Golden Wedding. Our brother, Benjamin Price, and sister Jane, his wife, requested their friends and relatives to meet them at the house of their son, Dr. Jacob Price, in West Chester, to celebrate the fiftieth anniversary of their marriage. We did not attend, as I was at the time indisposed, but a very large company convened, among them several of our children and grandchildren, who report it a season of much enjoyment. I wrote them a letter on the occasion, of which the following is a copy:

TO RACHEL L. PRICE.

I should have replied, my beloved niece, much sooner to thy interesting letter respecting the "Anniversary

Meeting," had not brother Jacob's agreeable though brief visit in some degree lessened the necessity, as I was convinced he understood the difficulty to me of such an excursion at present, and that I can only be with you in spirit; but that is a privilege that demands our sincere gratitude. To-day I have hardly had an idea that was not connected with you; not particularly the pleasure in anticipation, but in calling up the "dim and shadowy past." The present we are told is only ours, but the past I also claim; "The joys I have possessed, in spite of fate, are mine," and retrospection seems at this time my main engagement, as I am writing the autobiography, which I mentioned to thee in a late letter, that is now nearly completed.

How vividly since I took up my pen has the remembrance of the festival you meet to commemorate glided before my fancy, and how well do I remember every incident of that happy day, a lovelier that delicious season never afforded! The locusts, as if they knew of and wished to increase the general harmony, rung forth their notes on every passing breeze,—more distinctly heard, as we dined in the open air. Now you will not have their music, but far dearer to the principal actors in this drama of life will be the beloved tones of filial affection.

A feeling of pain crosses my mind as I reflect how many that were with us then will not now be visibly present, but am consoled by the remembrance that they await us in that happier sphere to which we are rapidly advancing.

I have been vainly conjecturing how many of the former

company will gladden your eyes again. Sister Margaret, whom I saw for the first time on that occasion, will, I trust, be with you now, and it will be a high gratification to her social nature to meet so many relatives and friends.

Sarah Carmalt, too, I well remember in that olden circle, and should love to meet again,—we have known more of life and its unfoldings, and would feel there were stronger ties between us than in our earlier days.

With Eli K. Price I made but slight acquaintance half a century ago, but in our interviews since have made up the deficiency, and not meeting him there is quite a large item in my regrets that I cannot attend the anniversary gathering.

The mention of his name revives the recollection of one remembered so tenderly, sadly, and long, and my feelings impel me to dwell for a brief space on the impression made by her first visit to us in company with Deborah Bringhurst.

Father was charmed with D—— because she so much in person, mind, and manners resembled a favorite sister, long since passed to the higher life.

I was equally delighted with Anna E. Price, perhaps for a better reason, our having so much in common. Every circumstance of that sweet visit is engraven on my memory. She accompanied us to our mid-week meeting; it was silent, as regards vocal communication, but its silence was eloquent to us, for she told Thomas and myself that she never experienced such heavenly feelings in any congregation.

It was a cool autumnal day, a steady breeze rattled the

casement and drifted the falling leaves against the window in front of us in profuse showers and all their many-colored hues. She compared the music of the wind to the Æolian harp, and the very same idea was engrossing my own mind. We repeated in concert an address to the Æolian harp, of which I now recollect but the last verse,—

> "Harp of the wind, the gates of Heaven
> Might surely move to sound like thine,
> And hope display in shades of even
> The spirit's flight to realms Divine."

I told Anna that to a mind constituted as hers the very breath of Heaven seemed poetry, and music, and perfume.

With Philip Price I have had less acquaintance than with any I have named, but he made us a very pleasant visit in the early part of our married life.

He read to us the "Lights and Shadows of Scottish Life," which I had never before seen, and have not since met with.

We had many years after a visit from his Matilda and her two daughters; she seemed to us the personification of gentleness and truth, and was all I expected to find her from my son, S. J. Paxson's, description. He used to apply to her the lines by Fitz-Greene Halleck,—

> "None knew her but to love her,
> None named her but to praise."

He spoke of her to me during the sickness that terminated his life, and his eldest daughter is named Helen Matilda.

To the brother and sister who are favored in age to call around them the dear ones of earlier days, I offer my heartfelt congratulations; they can look back upon a long and well-spent life in which they have been anxious to lay up the only wealth that will be available in the ceaseless ages of Eternity.

Rich in life's best treasures, children whose dutiful attention has rewarded them for their care in childhood, and now adds many a bright tint to their wintery sunset.

I have mentioned five of the Price family who will probably be in this interesting group. Of the Paxson family, the number was originally larger, but there will be fewer in attendance now, as all but three of fifteen have passed to the spirit world. One, however, who was not of the former wedding company will adorn the present one. She comes to us with a sister's claims, and justly beloved by us all. Long may she live, an ornament to society and a blessing to our brother.

"Your Fathers, where are they? And the Prophets, do they live forever?"

A host of memories awoke with this passage, but I cannot record them here, neither is it needful; their virtues have been commemorated by the hand of filial affection, and for the light of a younger generation their footprints yet remain uneffaced by the lapse of passing years.

A. J. P.

Since I commenced copying the foregoing I

received a letter from Lydia H., wife of our
nephew, Isaiah Price; it gives a pretty full account of the anniversary meeting, and will be
read with pleasure by all who are interested in
the subject.

My dear Aunt,—When thy granddaughter, Mary, asked
me to "write very soon, and tell grandmother about the
golden wedding," I meant that the request should receive
immediate attention, but a pressure of care before the occasion and company since have made me defer it till this
morning. I am at present at brother Paxson Price's pleasant
home feasting on strawberries, but that does not make me
forget my duty to thee. I am sorry I cannot send thee a
more vivid account, but as some compensation, I will send
thee Ann Preston's beautiful poetry and Cousin Ann Paschal's, who I think thee knows, also very pretty and appropriate.

In the first place, I can safely pronounce the whole affair
a great success, except the absence of thyself and dear
Uncle Thomas, which left quite a blank. I looked regret-
fully at your vacant places and pictured the deep poetic
language of thy eyes, could I have met their glances on
that eventful day; but I felt your spirit's sympathy and
thought with comforting assurance of that golden reunion
wherein the infirmities of the flesh would have no power
to divide us.

The day was very favorable, for had the sun shone as

warm as on the following day, the young people could not so much have enjoyed the social groups that collected so joyously under the spreading trees.

It was thought best for father and mother to remain in their chamber till the hour for meeting arrived, leaving the greeting with friends till after the ceremonies were over. They looked charmingly, and appeared pleased with themselves, each other, and all the numerous throng of relatives assembled there.

Mother was the first to break the solemn silence, and impressively said how good it was to be there, and called us all home to the truth as made manifest in our hearts by the Light that "lighteth every man that cometh into the world." Dr. Price then read an interesting narrative of their childhood and youth, of their happy home, and the watchful care that encircled them with loving influences within its blessed precincts, with allusions to the incidents and sports of those happy days. He concluded by saying, that though they had not accumulated much of this world's goods, they had laid up treasures of a more enduring character.

Then Uncle Eli K. Price read an original article of a touching and interesting character. I cannot pretend to give an account of its deep pathos; perhaps the impressive manner in which he read it added to the effect. His feelings almost overcame him during the recital, as he spoke of the companions all had been called upon to part with, except his brother Benjamin.

Then Ann Preston read her beautiful and appropriate

poetic tribute, also Ann Paschal's verses for the same occasion, and still there was another treat in reserve which I knew not of,—the reading of thy deeply interesting letter, which I need not enlarge upon further than to say thy spirit seemed brought very near to me, and no doubt to other appreciative hearts, when sister Rachel read those words of happy, loving import.

I was then called upon to read "The Old Man and his Bride." I could not do it justice: my voice faltered, and I fear I was not extensively heard.

Then Benjamin P. Wilson read the certificate. It was brief and to the purpose, and one hundred and sixty-nine names were appended.

Next thronged the guests to salute the happy pair, on whom all eyes were turned, and who on that 12th of June were perhaps the recipients of more heartfelt love and interest than on the day fifty years before, when their youthful love was plighted and the untried future was all before them, with its solemn responsibilities.

And now, if thee can descend from the heartfelt and enduring to that which perisheth, the table so richly adorned with fruits, flowers, and good things in abundance should claim some share of attention; at least it certainly did that day. All were invited to pass through the dining-room to see the table in its pristine beauty, and then ascend the back stairs into the chambers, hall, and sitting-room to be served by the waiters, and all were amply provided for.

In the afternoon we were invited to see cut the large cake that contained the ring, which, when discovered, was immediately placed on mother's finger, and there was quite a rush to see how it looked in its unwonted sphere.

Photographs were taken of the whole company, and of family groups, but they are not very good ; the artist came too late, and the day was cloudy.

I was sorry Edward M. and Mary C. Paxson were not present, and many shared in that regret, and expressed it.

I was glad Albert and Lavinia were with us, as it gave her an opportunity of meeting so many of her husband's kindred that she probably had seldom seen, and Cousin Mary Anna, whom I liked so much when I visited you last, and should be so pleased to know more of, I hardly exchanged a word with.

I regret that I did not see Cousin Mary P. Brown and her husband before they left. I had no conversation with him, and loving her so dearly made me wish to increase my interest in her companion.

The presents I had like to have forgotten, but I cannot enumerate them here ; suffice it to say they were many, various, and valuable, and mostly of a character suited to the age of the recipients.

Thy loving niece,

LYDIA H. PRICE.

I have just returned (Sixth month, 1867) from a visit to the home of my childhood, after a rather protracted absence, as I leave my present abiding place less frequently than in former days.

It is now owned by George G. and Sarah Maris, and their taste has added some new features to its beauty. Yet I confess that to my eyes one charm has passed away; three of the venerable elms planted by father's hand more than eighty years ago have fulfilled the prediction I made regarding them twenty years since, in a poetic address to my friends, the Magoffins, then residing there; a prediction very sure to be verified when we reflect that change is written upon all earthly things.

Ossian says, "The oaks of the mountains fall, the mountains themselves decay with years," and a part of the assertion we have all seen realized; therefore cannot reasonably expect these old elms to escape their doom, "Since hastens all nature to final decay." They are endeared to my feelings by a life-long association, for though I left that location so early, I have been intimate with all the subsequent inhabitants, which has not suffered my interest in the place to decline; it has been kept up perhaps as much by this influence, as being so closely entwined with early recollections.

I will copy, as a tribute to their memory, that

portion of the poem alluded to that relates to them :

Dear native shades, I greet your sylvan bowers,
Familiar in gay childhood's sunny hours,
As yet erect, in lofty pride ye stand,
Nor feel the weight of time's all-conquering hand.
Ye dread no blighting day, but come it must;
Your leafy honors prostrate in the dust.
As little reck the changes years have made
To those once dwelling in your grateful shade :
Ah! what fond ties asunder have been torn
Since first the sunlight on your brow was worn!
Youth's glossy locks, and age with silvery hair,
Manhood's firm step, and lisping childhood fair,
Have burst the bonds the immortal soul that bound,—
Wanderers in earth's wide waste, their home is found.

Home of my earliest joys,—that rural glade,—
Not all the changes times and taste have made
Can visions bright from memory's page dispel,
Of scenes remembered long and loved so well.
Your arching boughs the lawn still shadows o'er,
The brook still murmurs by the friendly door.
Though many an after-scene should be forgot,
My heart will linger in this lovely spot,
And still the light by faithful memory cast,
Like moonlight lustre, gild the blissful past.

"Scenes of the past, ye stand arrayed,
In thought, before my longing eye;
In all the change of sun and shade,
I see the visioned landscape lie."

Among the many auxiliaries to happiness provided for us by indulgent Providence, hope and memory seem to stand pre-eminent. Hope is the radiant star that lights life's early morning. Memory, the moonlight lustre that gilds its decline. Both have rendered me essential service through life, as they have strewn my pathway with unfading flowers.

I cannot say with a certain aged poet, "That all my treasures are with memory now," though her ministrations are more important to us in age than in our early days. It is true that many whose lives are protracted outlive their comforts and their friends; but I still have much to be grateful for, much to enjoy, and all the capacity for enjoyment remaining. I have recently returned from a visit to our granddaughter, whose marriage was lately spoken of in this book, and know not that my amount of pleasure would have been greater had I numbered only half my years.

It introduced me to several phases of life, all of which had their different attractions. The young, who had just commenced life's devious, and often eventful journey, with all their hopes yet before them, and those who had reared a large family of children, claiming and deserving a parent's pride and love, and who themselves afford an evidence that

> " The love that has battled with cares and tears
> Through springs and summer of passing years,"

is more engrossing and entire than when first pledged in early youth.

Several children are married and settled near them, and three lovely daughters still grace their home. Such is the family of John and Margaret Brown, of Mount Holly.

Their eldest daughter, Hannah, who is married to Andrew Fort, is an ornament to her sex. Fortunately, her husband, a man of talents and merit, fully appreciates her rare character, and I never saw more congeniality than exists between this admirable pair. Our beloved Mary P. Brown we found well and happy in her pleasant and commodious home. She considers, and

with reason, that her lines have fallen in pleasant places.

> Her husband, all Hope's pencil bright could paint;
> Youth's early dreams must seem a picture faint
> Of all the virtues that adorn his mind,—
> His manners manly, gentle, frank, and kind,
> His heart by nature formed on liberal plan,
> Embued with love to God and love to man.
> Such is the friend her destiny who sways;
> Heaven grant them peace and length of blissful days.

A character so in unison with her own must·
insure domestic happiness.

After two weeks delightfully spent with them
we returned to our home, which never lost
ground by comparison with other places, however beautiful and attractive. We had, while
absent, seen the part of New Jersey generally
considered the garden of the State, and it had
its full portion of deserved admiration; but
when we came in sight of Lahaska Mountain,
then illumined by the setting sun, and beheld
from its summit the fertile valley extended at its
base, I remembered and felt the truth of Albert
S. Paxson's descriptive lines,—

Though loftier summits greet morn's radiant glow,
They shadow not a lovelier vale below;
Not Eden, in her earliest bloom arrayed,
Surpassed the beauty of this charming glade.

My own residence, improved and adorned as
it now is by Edward's taste, has no superior in
the valley. It will probably be my home while
an earthly home is needed, which cannot be very
long after seventy-six years.

But to some other loving hearts
  May all this beauty be
The dear retreat, the Eden home,
  That it has been to me.

A THANKSGIVING.

For the morning's ruddy splendor,
  For the noontide's radiant glow,
For the golden smile of sunset,
  Illuming all below;
For flowers, those types of Eden,
  That gem the virgin sod,
And seem to ope their petals
  To tell us of our God.

They flood the silent wilderness
  With beauty and perfume;
They bloom around our pathway,
  They blossom on the tomb;

They are alphabets of angels,
   Though written on the sod,
And if man would read them wisely,
   Might lead his soul to God.

For the spring, with all its promise,
   For the summer's boundless store,
For autumn's richer treasures,
   And the winter's wilder roar;
For the joyous evening fireside,
   By thought and feeling awed,
For the loving hearts around it,
   I thank Thee, oh, my God.

For the memories that encircle
   The happy days gone by;
For the holy aspirations
   That lift the soul on high;
For the hope, in brighter regions,
   By seraph footsteps trod,
To meet the lost and loved ones,
   I thank Thee, oh, my God.

Tenth month, 1867.

When I laid down my pen at the conclusion of
the last chapter I had no expectation of resum-
ing it, at least so far as this book was concerned;
but as an interesting epoch of our lives is almost
at hand, one which comes to few, and but once

to any, I have concluded to commit to paper some of my thoughts and feelings on the occasion for our children, and possibly some others who have known and loved us may glance over it with interest.

Should we live one week more, we shall have attained the fiftieth anniversary of our married life. The present day seems to bring up before me all the events of the one so far in the distance. The locality is the same and the weather is similar as possible, affording efficient aid to memory.

We spent some hours on the summit of Lahaska Mountain. The scenery was new to my Philadelphia friends, and its wild beauty could not but attract their admiration,—

> "There was a glory in the air,
> A mellow lustre in the sky."

It was Indian summer, to me the loveliest season of the year. The woodlands were tinged with all the colors of the rainbow,—just enough of green remaining to gratify the eye fond of variety, but not to identify it as the original color. Now, as I view it from the window where I write, it wears the same bright garb as half a century ago, and I can hardly believe that so long a period has elapsed since the morning succeeding our wedding, when we rambled o'er it with that young and happy bridal group.

All these memories have to me an almost sacred import, now that the larger number who shared them with me are inhabitants of a holier sphere, and I have recollected, in connection with the subject, some expressions of a late attractive writer: "I go out upon the October hills and question the genii of the woods, 'How does the leaf fade?' Grandly, magnificently, imperially, so that the glory of its coming is eclipsed by the glory of its departure. Thus the forests make answer to-day."

And thus does my heart make answer when I contemplate the analogy between the fading leaf and the change that awaits us all,—

> What a world of thought and feeling
> Might those fifty years unfold;
> Joys with which no stranger mingled,
> Sorrows that were never told.

The sorrows, I acknowledge with reverential gratitude, have been as few as are compatible with a state of being where good and evil are blended, doubtless in wisdom, for our eternal benefit.

But our joys have been numerous and constantly mingled with our daily life. May our thankfulness be a deep and heartfelt emotion, in some degree proportionate to the munificence of the blessings so liberally dispensed to us.

The motto of the sun-dial, "I mark only the hours that shine," I always admired, and perhaps it suited our natural temperament, and I think it is only justice to ourselves to say, that it has materially contributed to brighten our lives by often substituting the sunshine for the shadow,—

> "And garlanding with fairy skill
> The milestones of our way."

Tenth month, 1867.

Our fiftieth anniversary was the 22d of this month, and will, I doubt not, be a memorable day to those assembled at our Woodlawn home on that occasion. We had not expected to have any company except our children and grandchildren, but an arrangement was made by some of our friends and relatives to meet here on that day to celebrate our golden wedding.

It might well be termed a "surprise" party, as neither my husband nor myself knew of the plan; had I seen the large wreathed cake with the inscription on its coat of sugar, the "Fiftieth Anniversary," brought the night before by E. M. P. and his wife, I had not probably remained in ignorance of the pleasure in store for us. The eventful 22d dawned in unusual beauty; a few clouds flitted over its early morning, but dispersed long before noonday,—emblematic of many a life's journey, and the very counterpart of that day which, half a century ago, saw us united in bonds that only death can sever.

Before the forenoon was half gone by, and while my daughter, Mary C. Paxson, in capacity of bridesmaid, assisted me in attiring to meet the little family party I expected to see, several carriages drove into the lawn; upon inquiring the meaning, I was told that it might be a surprise party, as they had become quite a common occurrence lately. When we went down-stairs, we found West Chester, Philadelphia, Abington, and Newtown represented in our parlors, at which my amazement was only equalled by my delight. About sixty persons were assembled, our nieces and nephews composing the larger number.

Several letters and essays were brought us during the morning, and it was concluded to read them before the guests left the table, which was accordingly done; at the close of this ceremony came the most delightful surprise of all: E. M. P. read us a poem which only his wife knew he had written. It took a comprehensive, yet condensed view of family events of the last half-century; many of these appealed so forcibly to the feelings of his hearers that the effect seemed electrical. Most of them knew something of the persons so graphically portrayed, and could thereby make some estimate of the correctness of the picture. A copy was so generally requested, and so earnestly, that the writer had it printed for distribution among them.

I will transcribe it here, as it certainly contributed more than any other incident to that day's enjoyment:

Awake, my muse, thy slumbering lyre,—
With happy thoughts my pen inspire;

For fifty years of joys and pain
Repeat themselves to-day again.
And those who in their early youth
Pledged to each other love and truth,
Pause in their journey o'er life's way
For love and sympathy to-day.
The vows that fifty years ago
Were whispered, lovingly and low,
Are yet as fresh as in that hour
When love first felt his youthful power;
And though their locks are silvered o'er,
And youth's quick pulse they feel no more;
Though feeble steps now mark their way
Adown the fast declining day;
The heart has lost not of its youth,—
Their love has lost not of its truth,
But rich in all that makes life sweet,
To-day their friends and kindred meet;
And as we mingle round the board,
And share the cheer with which it's stored,
We'll note the shadows flitting fast,—
The shadows of the silent past.

And first, of that ancestral home,
Where fifty years ago there shone
Upon the happy guests around
The light of happiness profound.
For there a cherished grandsire stood,
Of noble mien and happy mood;

His locks, though slightly tinged with gray,
Were ample, and were brushed away
From the broad forehead smooth and high,
Beneath which shòne the kindling eye,—
The index of that genial heart,—
A stranger to the guiles of art,
A very patriarch was he,
As, standing by his own roof-tree,
He made thrice welcome those who came
To share with them the rustic game,
Or join in social converse dear
Of what befell the passing year.
Nor was his genius all confined
To matters of a rustic kind;
A modest muse he early won,
And when his daily task was done,
His lyre he touched with ready skill,—
Its notes come trembling to us still.
And by his side with stately mien
The partner of his life is seen;
With cultured grace, and carriage free,
In all that makes a queen was she.
And yet upon that classic face
A tinge of sadness we may trace;
For one whose steps in childhood's hours,
Along life's bright and happy bowers,
She long had watched with tender care,
Now stood in bridal vestments there;

Another claimed her youthful heart,—
The mother from her child must part;
Yet he to whom was freely given
The best and choicest gift of Heaven,
Amid the guests in that old hall,
Now proudly stood the peer of all.
And as the solemn vows were spoken,
Of trusting faith, the fitting token,
Their lives, diverging until then,
Unite, and open not again.

Of other scenes I now will sing,—
To Walnut Grove our guests will bring,—
Where first in childhood's hours there
A mother watched with tender care
The footsteps of her darling boys,—
The choicest of her earthly joys.
Or, with a filial love that shone
In every word, and look, and tone,
Her aged parents' pathway smoothed,—
Their sufferings and their sorrows soothed.
And as their fast declining sun
Showed that their course was nearly run,
With holy love watched by their side,
As up their gentle spirits glide
To join the happy throng, who sing
Hosannas to the Heavenly King.
And thus we see our mother's life,
In her young years a constant strife,

To know how much of it could be
Laid as a gift, unsought and free,
Upon that altar, raised above
All others, to her filial love.
May we who meet around her here,
To greet her on her fiftieth year
Of wedded bliss, take well to heart
The lesson which such lives impart;
And make her feel that not in vain
Her bread was cast upon the main,
But that in years it will return
To bless her in her brief sojourn
On earthly scenes, and light her way
To regions of eternal day.

And thus the years sped on apace;
The old farm-house, with quiet grace,
Nestled among the dear old hills,
Adown whose sides the sparkling rills
Went singing onward on their way,
Or turned our mimic wheels in play.
The rolling seasons brought to each
The lessons which the seasons teach,—
The changing leaf, the fading life,
The swelling bud, the earnest strife,
The winter's snow, the village school,
The solemn teacher on his stool,
With pen put back behind his ear,
The well-used rod, too, always near;

A sovereign in his little realm,
He guides with steady hand the helm.
Of childish sports we had our share:
For birds we set the crafty snare;
Lured the meek hare with cunning art,—
Ah! well each one performed his part.
And when the blasts of winter came,
And icy fetters bound the main,
With skates well fastened on our feet,
We lightly skimmed the frozen sleet;
Then, when the shades of night came on,
And lowly sank the winter's sun,
The lowing herds, with faithful care,
Were sheltered from the piercing air.
The chores done up, each one betook
Himself to game or pleasant book;
Or gathered round the kitchen hearth,
The scene of joyous, quiet mirth:
And as the wintry wind swept by,
Piling the snow-flakes up on high
In curling drifts around the door,
Or blowing in upon the floor,
The crackling fire was freshly stirred;
The blasts without were scarcely heard,
As up the chimney's mighty throat
The flame and cinders lightly float.
The wood, piled on with generous hand,
The huge back log and fiery brand

Light up the room, and o'er the wall
Fantastic shadows gently fall.
And then the weird tale of ghosts,
Of heroes, and of mighty hosts
That met in battle's shock afar ;
The thunders of the mighty war
That rocked our country, when the sun
Of Freedom rose at Lexington.
And when the winter's tale was o'er,
And lessons conned with trouble sore,
The store of nuts was gayly sought,
The steaming mug of cider brought,
The golden apples from the bin,
And doughnuts our contentment win ;
And thus in pleasure's pleasant ways
Were passed our childhood's happy days.

And now—we speak of later things—
Each rolling year its story brings :
Our parents now sit down alone
At Woodlawn, their new mountain home.
Their sons have each a daughter brought
To share their mother's every thought ;
And children's children come to cheer
The grandsire's heart from year to year.
Ah ! would that only blessings grew,
And sorrows vanished with the dew.
But other themes to us are given ;
We take them as decrees of Heaven.

A shadow flits across the hearth,—
A spirit pure has left the earth ;
A wife in all that makes the name,—
Our loss is her eternal gain.
And now again the shadows fall,—
Once more we have the funeral pall,
And Death's pale rider stops before
Our eldest brother's open door ;
And in the early days of spring
We hear the startling summons ring.
Ah ! well he met that fearful call,—
Resigned, and calm amid it all ;
Relying on that Faith which gave
To him the victory o'er the grave.

And now once more the month is here
That strews the Autumn's lonely bier
With falling leaves and dying flowers,
Fit emblems of this world of ours.
The sunlight and the shadows fall
On stream and vale and storied hall ;
The mountain rears its solemn crest,
The wild bird wings him to his nest,
The Wolf-Rocks stand out bold and clear,—
Little reck they the dying year.
The soft winds linger through the pines,—
They sing the songs of other times ;
The barns well filled with winter's store,
Enough for use and for the poor ;

While on the breeze is borne along
The merry husker's cheerful song.
And Woodlawn on this happy day,
Robed in autumnal vestments gay,
A greeting kind extends to all
Who meet here at affection's call.
And as we separate to-day,
May each one as he goes away
Take with him in his happy heart
The lessons which such scenes impart,
And not forget that day by day
Our lives are flitting fast away ;
Our bark is speeding to that shore
Where kindred have gone on before.

With E. M. P. and Mary C. P. came her mother, Rachel H. Newlin, to our anniversary meeting, and she, with her children, remained here two days after the celebration. She visited the farm on which her youth was passed, and had the pleasure of narrating to her sister, Hannah Howell, with whom she then resided, all the incidents of those pleasantly spent days. One day only, after her return home, was permitted them for this happy intercourse and tranquil enjoyment, before her almost idolized sister was summoned to a holier sphere, for which the

29

purity of her earthly life had prepared her redeemed spirit.

The particulars of her death, received from
our daughter, M. C. P., are so full of interest,
and indeed admonition, as they so loudly speak
the language, "Be ye also ready," that I will
give the letter containing the account a place
here, knowing it must be read with deep interest
by all whose eyes shall meet these pages:

PHILADELPHIA, Nov. 6, 1867.

MY DEAR MOTHER,—Has thee wondered at not hearing
from me? I had thought thee would, and yet I have not felt
that I could write thee of the startling dispensation which
has fallen upon us. I think the very first direction I gave to
Edward was "write to mother," and I know that it was done,
and that thy tender, sympathizing heart would feel for us
as only few out of our own immediate family would know
how to feel. Oh! mother, what a light has gone from our
hearts and homes! gone in the twinkling of an eye, leaving
us bewildered and wondering. How magnanimous and
noble and gentle and good she was, how filled with all the
spirit graces, none who knew her can ever forget. Generous in hospitality, and cordial in sympathy, she became
the benefactor of many and the friend of all. If there was
exhibited one trait of disposition more prominently than
another, it was her delicate consideration for the feelings of

others. The last words that fell from her loving lips were a fitting illustration of this. Having remained up later that evening than usual, she turned to Cousin Mary Allibone, who slept with her, and said, "Dear, I must get into the habit of retiring earlier, it keeps thee up too late," bade her sweetly good-night, and we know not when she awoke again, or when she passed to Heaven. In the early morning sister Hetty went softly into her room for something, and saw her sitting on the chair beside her bed; her right arm was lying over the arm of the chair, her left hand laid upon her breast, with her head reclining a little over the left shoulder, just as though she had fallen asleep there. Cousin Mary was just rising from the other side of the bed; in a moment they were beside her. Ma, who had returned from market, was coming quietly up the stairs lest she should wake her, when a cry of terror smote upon her ear; she ran hastily into the room. In vain they strove to revive her; it might have been several hours since her pure spirit had gone forth, we may never know. But we do know that she rests in peace, and that our hearts are made sorrowful.

I wish, dear mother, thee could have seen her ere they laid her away, she looked so very lovely. Not a line of age or care marked her beautiful brow, and upon her radiant countenance there shone celestial peace. It seemed as though her "lost youth had been given back," and as if we were permitted a glimpse of that new body in which the immortal spirit was to be clothed; all who saw her were wonderfully impressed with this remarkable change.

She who in life had never given pain to any, passed without pain to the reward of the just.

Our dear mother is overwhelmed with this blow. I scarce know what to tell thee about her.

Thee knows how their hearts were bound together, until they seemed to live but one life. How now can she bear up alone? We will do all we can to sustain and gently comfort her. Will thee not, dear mother, aid us by thy sympathy? It will be very grateful to her.

She seems to reproach herself for the few days of absence, spent so pleasantly with you, standing, as she says, "on the brink of a precipice and knowing it not. Oh, why did she go?" But we try to tell her that she went in obedience to Auntie's wish, as well as her own, and point to the pleasure she enjoyed in the recital of every minute particular of that happy fiftieth anniversary, and our pleasant and probably last ride to and around the "old place," which was the scene of their childhood's recollections. I wanted to read to her, above all others, Edward's Anniversary Poem. Seventh day morning was fixed upon for my doing so. I let mother tell her, but no one else, about it, and I was to go up and surprise them all with it. She seemed disappointed I could not come on Sixth day, but when mother told her why, she replied, "Oh, well, then, Seventh day will do. She will come early, and we will have a nice morning together in Hetty's room." I went early, but the dear one whom we loved to honor had been called hence by the angels, and had taken her place amid the company of Heaven.

M. C. P.

Written for the fiftieth anniversary of the wedding-day of Thomas and Ann J. Paxson, by Ann Preston :

'Tis the soft and rich October,
   'Tis the time of golden haze;
Golden maples, weddings golden,
   Well befit these golden days.

With the grace Lahaska Mountain
   Dons its robe of richest hue,
Have the soft, warm tints of autumn,
   Friends beloved, been laid on you?

And while nearer ones are bringing,
   In their love, what gifts they may,
I would drop this little leaflet
   As my token for the day.

You have made my summer richer
   By the seeds your hands have strewn;
Something in your life and spirit
   Has become in part my own.

You have offered gifts of beauty
   In a life so glad and sweet,
That beholders, with thanksgiving,
   Walk their way with firmer feet.

We, the undersigned, relatives and friends of Thomas and Ann J. Paxson, assembled at their residence at Woodlawn Farm, Buckingham Township, Bucks County, Pennsylvania, on the 22d day of the Tenth month, 1867, to celebrate their golden wedding, or fiftieth anniversary of their marriage, have on this joyous occasion subscribed our names to this paper in memoriam. The said Thomas and Ann J. Paxson having first attached their signatures:

	Thomas Paxson.
	Ann J. Paxson.
John M. Comly.	Albert S. Paxson.
Mary Ann Comly.	Lavinia S. Paxson.
Ellwood Tyson.	Edward M. Paxson.
Hannah Ann Tyson.	Mary C. Paxson.
Elizabeth Paxson.	Mary Anna Paxson.
Sarah Tyson.	J. Hart Bye.
Agnes T. Paxson.	Helen M. Bye.
Rebecca Pickering.	R. Howell Brown.
Emmeline M. Tyson.	Mary P. Brown.
Tacie F. Tyson.	Carrie W. Paxson.
Anna M. Tyson.	Edward Ely Paxson.
Lizzie H. Tyson.	Harry Douglass Paxson.
Henry Paxson.	Harriet P. Janney.
Charles Comly.	Jane J. Philips.
Anna L. Comly.	Sidney K. Furman.
John T. Comly.	Joshua W. Paxson.
Anna E. Comly.	Ettie Janney.
Jacob C. Paxson.	Marie P. Furman.
Eliza A. Paxson.	Samuel J. Pickering.
Philip Paxson.	Rachel H. Newlin.

Helen F. Paxson.	Rebecca Ely.
Rachel Paxson.	Mary Smith.
Carrie Philips.	Debbie Ann Morris.
Fannie Janney.	Emma L. Stackhouse.
William W. Morris.	Fannie Smith.
Roseanna S. Morris.	

I had in the Eleventh month, 1868, a dream of rather unusual significance, which some of my friends wished me to commit to paper. I seemed, in Dreamland, to meet with a relative and friend of early days. It could not be termed a conversation, as the recital he gave me and requested me to write I do not recollect interrupting by any question or observation. I will give his own language, which, I believe, I correctly remember.

THE COMMUNICATION.

I have lately been informed that thee has been writing "Memoirs of the Johnson Family," and am induced to furnish materials for another memory, yet without flattering myself that the narrative will compare in interest with the account of those worthy and gifted ones whom thee has been memorializing. But my story may not be without its use. Even the wanderings of my way may serve as a beacon light to warn some unwary traveller of the dangers that beset his path and enable him to choose the safer way. I need not, to one who has known me from my childhood and youth, speak of my early advantages. Blest with parents of brilliant talents and undeviating integrity, who enjoyed the confidence of so many good as well as gifted persons, my home could not be other than a school for morality and religion, as well as general knowledge, and I delighted in the literary converse our house afforded, even when a child. When I was seventeen I united myself with a literary society of which I was the youngest member. I was invited to deliver an address, and accepted the invitation. They were pleased with it and requested a copy for publication. I consented, without the knowledge of my parents, and many pamphlets were printed. My young companions all applauded, and even my father paid me some compliments on the occasion, but not so my mother. She considered it the dawning of genius, yet was not pleased to see me so early brought to the bar of criticism, and probably thought that the fondness for notoriety which it fostered might have injurious effects on my opening character.

When I was nineteen I formed an attachment for a young woman who lived near my residence, who was sensible, amiable, and bewitchingly fair.. She was domestic in her habits and tastes, and seemed to possess every requisite

"Well-ordered home man's best delight to make."

But my friends objected; I was young and had not made my mark in life; I had not then chosen my occupation. My father was a successful merchant, and, as I was his eldest son, wished to take me into partnership with him, but my partiality for the legal profession made me averse

to his proposal, and he at length gave up his preference
for mine. This interposed an objection to an early marriage, as it might probably be a long time ere I was in a
situation to support a wife, but had I settled then, young
as I was, it might have had a saving influence on my after-
life. She would have been an anchor, and prevented my
being tossed without stability by the waves of life. About
my twentieth year I commenced the study of law with the
brightest anticipations, because I viewed myself on the
direct road to fame and fortune, though the latter had, with
one of my temperament, less weight than the former consideration. I completed my studies in as short a time as
any of my cotemporaries, and entered upon my untried
sphere of practice with pleasure and alacrity.

But often vain are human calculations, and especially so
when they have not their foundation in reason. Of this
character were mine, for I longed to rise to eminence in
my profession at once ; I was conscious of intellect superior
to the plodding young lawyers by whom I was surrounded,
and saw with bitterness some of them reach earlier the goal
I had so anxiously sought to attain, though my success would
have satisfied any one of less inordinate ambition. To
drown my disappointment I had in an evil hour recourse
to the inebriating bowl, and from that hour I date succeeding years of bitter sorrow and degradation. I will pass
over these lightly ; often did I wish they could be forever
obliterated from memory, for they were neither "pleasing
to God nor useful to mankind." At length I married, and
took my wife home to reside with my parents, where she

was treated with great kindness, with which compassion must have largely mingled.

In less than two years after this event my excellent and gifted mother was taken from us. She had lived to see her fond hopes blighted as regards her darling son, but not to see my reformation, and during all the following years the pangs of remorse were my constant companions from the reflection that she might truly adopt the language,—

"Thou, thou, my son, wert my disease and death."

My wife then took charge of my father's establishment to his entire satisfaction, in which station she continued till his death. He did not live either to see my return to usefulness, happiness, and respectability, and in consequence left my portion of his fortune in the care of a trustee. This was to me very humiliating, and seemed for a time to increase my habits of dissipation; but after I overcame these I saw the justice and wisdom of the arrangement, and a deeper humiliation succeeded that I had given the occasion. And now I come to a brighter page of my life's history, which I know will afford thee pleasure, as thee never entirely lost thy interest in me; of this thee gave evidence by giving my name to thy gifted son in honor of our early friendship.

I was sitting one evening by my parlor fire in deep and bitter musing; memory recalled the noble form and placid face of my beloved brother, taken some years before from a lovely wife and three little daughters by that giant evil, intemperance. The last sad scene of his life came vividly before me; his deep contrition, his late regrets for time misspent and talents misapplied, his hope of mercy and forgiveness through his own penitence and a Saviour's love, all these crowded on my mind, and lastly, when we stood by his coffin, the voice of a female Friend broke the solemn silence by these words, "I seem to hear the anthem of the angels to greet a penitent and redeemed sinner." Then came up before me my own situation, what I had been, what I was now, and what I might have been.

The bitterness of such reflections no one who has not felt can possibly know. While my spirit was weighed down by these sombre thoughts, my wife and our two little children passed through the room. She said, pleasantly, "We are going to hear Lewis C. Levin lecture on temperance, will you not accompany us?" She had so often made the same request before without success that she had probably little confidence now, and I was almost surprised at myself; perhaps the train of meditation into which I had plunged had something to do with the result. Be that as it may, it was the happiest event of my life, and by which my whole after-career was guided. I hardly need say that the lecture was able and eloquent to those who know the effect on myself, and I felt disposed to address to him some lines of a living poet as very applicable:

> "Thy voice sounds like a Prophet's word,
> And in its solemn tones are heard
> The thanks of millions yet to be."

At the conclusion of the meeting I signed the pledge which has brightened my existence. Thee has heard me lecture, and express my resolve if life was spared to endeavor to compensate by my devotion to the cause for the evil influences of my example.

I sometimes had engagements for every day, a month in advance, and have the happy consciousness that many through my exertions have been turned from the error of their ways to a better and brighter life in the present world, and good grounds for hope of an inheritance in one that fadeth not away.

KENNETT SQUARE.

To A. J. P.

MY DEAR FRIEND,—Absent but not forgotten. In these glorious summer days, amid the voice of birds and the waving of trees, with the bluest of skies overhead, and the purest and sweetest of airs around me, I think of thee and of the letters received from thee,—the two most recent ones, respectively dated 6th and 7th month last. I have long deferred writing, because so many letters had accumulated to be answered in my summer vacation, many of them on business, that I have put off from time to time the prompting of the spirit to write.

I left the city six weeks ago. It has been many years since I have taken so much absolute rest, and the brightening up of olden ties is very pleasant. I have had delightful meetings with old friends, and have realized how inevitably people are themselves, despite of years.

Fifty is very much like twenty-five, except that in all true natures, when there has been opportunity of culture, there is an expanding and mellowing of feeling that makes the latter age more beautiful than the former. There are exceptions; hard circumstances, and ill-health operating on those whose vitality and energy were weak in the beginning, may overbear the beautiful in character and make the meridian tame, and the coming age "dark and unlovely;" but among my early friends the brighter pictures predominate.

Thy lines in regard to F. W. Harper are beautiful and appropriate. She is a woman of genius fitted to inspire the poet's lay. Perhaps it is because she is older and more mature, but to me she is a more attractive speaker than Anna D——; she warms my heart more, though she may be inferior in dramatic effect.

I was truly glad to hear of thy visit to Chester County. It may be true, as Whittier says, that nature is the same inspiring presence everywhere, that "he who sees his native brooks dance in the sun has seen them all." But still a ride in summer amid the varied scenery of our Bucks and Chester Counties is an enjoyment to awaken the spirit of thanksgiving.

I think I was never so impressed with the munificence of nature, the abounding richness of summer, the glorious beauty of our earth, as since I left the city. Already the plume of the golden-rod is blooming by the wayside, and the insect hum in the evening making the silence audible, suggests a contrast with the perpetual rumble of the city atmosphere. I fear I cannot visit you till autumn, if at all this year. I return to Philadelphia to-morrow, but after a few days there I hope to go on a visit to a brother who lives in Lancaster, and is the eldest of our family.

And now, my dear friend, I must say farewell; thy friendship has added to the fulness and richness of my life, and among the many blessings for which my heart overflows in thanksgiving is that of thy life and thy love.

ANN PRESTON.

Fifth month, 1870.

I find in my autobiography no record bearing date 1870, yet the year has not been devoid of incidents that might claim a notice from my pen.   ·

The latter part of its immediate predecessor was marked by a deep sorrow: R. Howell Brown, the husband of our granddaughter Mary, after many months of declining health, passed to the higher life. He was only in his twenty-eighth year, but

> "Innocence and virtue is the gray hair to man,
> And unspotted life is old age."

By this standard we may safely measure the brief term of his existence, as his course on earth from early days seemed a preparation for the future life, for it was marked by love to God and love to man, and its close was peaceful and happy. Though surrounded by the strongest ties that bind to life, a happy husband and father, he was prepared to exclaim, in sincerity of heart, "Gracious Father, I am ready, wilt Thou take my spirit home?" He quietly passed to his heavenly home Ninth month, 5th, 1869.

Soon after his death our granddaughter and her infant son, T. Howell Brown, came to reside with us at the dwelling where had been passed her childhood and early youth, adding by her presence comfort and joy to our declining years.

The following extracts are from letters received from my husband while I was in New Jersey, at R. H. Brown's, principally during his sickness:

BUCKINGHAM, 7th mo., 31st, 1869.

DEAR N.,—While sitting on the portico last evening with a feeling of loneliness and sadness upon my spirit, the words, "Yes, he is here," were gladly heard. It was Edward, accompanied by Albert, and, as the former and his wife had just returned from Lumberton, my anxiety to hear from you there was relieved.

I was very glad to hear so directly from Howell and

Mary; I feel a deep and abiding solicitude for their well-being every way, and, if favored with health, it has ever been my unwavering belief that, with their good impulses, their varied talents, and true integrity of purpose, they would continue to experience a partaking of the tree of Life daily, and thereby be as lights shining brighter and brighter to the perfect day. But we must leave all things to Him who "seeth not as man seeth;" and what matter it whether called hence early in life, or when bending with the weight of infirmities and years, when there has been an earnest care to have oil in our vessels, and our lamps trimmed and brightly burning?

How rapid is the flight of time! Summer seems little more than commenced, yet it will soon be numbered with the things that were. But those that have filled up the measure of their duty may feel that there is not much to regret.

Albert, Lavinia, and their two little boys this week joined an excursion party from Lambertville to New York, up the North River some distance, and returned at ten o'clock the same evening. What a day of progress is the present one! Let me hear from thee soon and often. I have been told you consider Howell rather improving. How agreeable to witness his patient amiability, which even sickness is not able to subdue; and the little T. Howell Brown, the sprightly, intelligent boy,—he must always have a place in thy reports. Adieu for the present, as it is near mail-time. How convenient it is, when we have nothing more to say, to lay the blame on the mail, which cannot defend itself! Often I suspect it has to bear the blame, when the real cause is dearth of material.

8th month, 3d, 1869.

BELOVED WIFE,—After supper last evening I set off for Albert's, supposing he would be at home from New Jersey by that time. I soon met dear little Harry with a letter from thee. We sat down together on the green bank by the road-side to read it; I then went on to Albert's. He was glad indeed that he had been with you, and seemed fully aware of the peaceful, heavenly atmosphere that pervades your abiding place. Rebecca Ely was much pleased with thy letter, which she handed me to read, and it opened an interesting conversation between us, and the evening passed along to mutual satisfaction.

Yesterday was our Monthly Meeting. After the business was disposed of, a printed document of twenty-seven pages was read, giving a very interesting account of the harmonious action of Friends of our six Yearly Meetings in America of the one part, and the President of the United States and his cabinet of the other. This was read to the assembly; after which a few remarks were made alluding to the peaceful and just policy pursued by William Penn towards the Indians two centuries ago, and has ever since been held sacred by both parties. Their attention was also directed to subsequent occasions wherein Friends have voluntarily interested themselves to arrest fraud practised upon those greatly wronged and comparatively defenceless people.

31

The arrival of Friends at the various destinations to which the government has appointed them has been joyfully hailed by the poor Red men of the forest. How far their action in this case may be successful is yet to be proved. It is a most arduous and responsible position, but the feeling of strict justice to all will be their guiding star.

I do all my writing on the portico this warm weather. I write upon our little mahogany stand of 1817 memory. What a lapse of happy years have we since seen together! And the beautiful stand is before me now, undefaced by spot or stain, yet what changes since then have we witnessed! Nearly all of our early friends, full of bloom, promise, and hope, have gone, we trust, to join the company of saints and angels who circle round the throne.

Extract from a letter dated Ninth month, 4th, 1869:

MY DEAR N.,—I saw Albert since his return from New Jersey, and though he does not bring tidings calculated to revive our drooping hopes as regards dear Howell, yet there is left us the consolation that though our beloved grandson may thus early be called away, that he is entirely resigned to the will of an all-wise Providence, and has known and experienced the power of redeeming love; this power has enabled him to say, "O death, where is thy sting? O grave, where is thy victory?"

Dear Mary, whose allotment may be life prolonged for a

season, may she look to the same Divine Power that is able to sustain through the most afflicting bereavements.

10th month, 10th, 1869.

This brings me up to my seventy-sixth year, and in twelve more days we shall see the fifty-second anniversary of our marriage,—both still enjoying pretty good health, and almost clear of the infirmities incident to advanced life.

Vegetation is here as green as in the spring, except the trees: their foliage has assumed their rich autumnal hue.

Thee will find in the *Bucks County Intelligencer* a notice of the death of Sarah, widow of Henry Smith; she enjoyed good health till within half an hour of her quiet departure hence. She is one of the few of thy early associates who have remained here so long, and her lot in life has always seemed a peculiarly happy one.

Thine affectionately,
THOMAS PAXSON.

Extract from a letter dated Eleventh month, 19th, 1870:

MY DEAR SISTER,—As I had made arrangements to be at home the day I left your place, I concluded to be on the alert early in the morning, otherwise my return would have been postponed for a day, and my call on my friend at Centreville accomplished. My walk and following ride in a chilly morning proved too much for me, and I have been confined to the house ever since I came home, but am improving, and hope in future not to attempt more than I can accomplish, for what would have been an easy task in earlier life is something of a risk after seventy-six years.

My late visit to your place was a very pleasant one, and as I found you both enjoying health so much better than I had anticipated, the reflection of the amount of happiness you are yet possessors of was of the most cheering kind.

It is so common to find persons of our age failing (as it is usually termed) even more in their intellectual than their physical powers, that when I meet with those who retain them all, and the freshness and vigor of thought characterizing their best days, I feel that a visit to them is a real intellectual pilgrimage; and I never make it but it reminds me of Barley-Wood, and the agreeable reminiscences connected with that time-honored place,

"Where taste would homage pay to mind."

I know from my own experience that it requires considerable mental effort to contend successfully against the paralyzing influences of declining years, and in order that my efforts may not be unavailing, I have adopted a system of study in addition to the other intellectual exercises of which I have spoken to thee. Every day when at home I read a few pages of Virgil or some other Latin author. This is done with the lexicon and Latin grammar at hand. By this plan I keep familiar not only with the meaning of the words, but the rules of the language, and the facilities of translating it into English. The same plan is pursued daily with my Greek Testament, and occasionally other writings in that language. These exercises, besides the consciousness they afford of some mental vigor, have this additional result, that in my visits to advanced schools where those languages are taught, I have satisfaction in listening to the exercises, and sometimes propounding questions to the pupils.

Among my literary pursuits is one connected with a periodical of Philadelphia, called the *School-Day Visitor*. It has a mathematical department, to which I have been for some time a contributor. The editor has solicited me to furnish some articles for an almanac to be connected with this work, and I consented.

This Annual will soon appear, and as I expect several copies, I will send thee one. It will contain some essays in which thee will feel an interest. I have lately been induced to take an English work, called the "Educational Times." It is published in London, and, besides its mathematics, is very valuable for its general literature. Among the latter is the cheap editions of Standard Authors noticed. Mostly they are very much condensed, and often sold for a few shillings. For instance, Boswell's Life of Johnson is comprised in one moderately-sized volume, and many of the works aim to give the beauties of the standard writers rather than the whole of their productions. I feel but little interest in these condensed publications, especially as those who make the selections too often give us what I should not term the beauties of the author, and in the book named it would be like the play of Hamlet without the "Prince of Denmark."

I will send thee the "Standard," containing one of W. Phillips' best efforts, but I must conclude.

Affectionately thy brother,
WILLIAM H. JOHNSON.

Extract of a letter from Matilda, wife of Stephen Rushmore, Old Westbury, Long Island, First month, 1871 :

MY DEAR FRIEND,—Scarcely a day has passed since thy kind letter was received but my heart has been turned towards thee with the salutation of love. Sickness, absence from home, and a pressure of care and company, each in turn, has absorbed the passing hour. It is long since we have met, but I have ever felt thee near to me in spirit. I used to indulge the hope that thee and thy worthy husband would visit us; but as the seasons came and went the expectation failed, but not the love, for, says the Apostle, " Love never faileth." Ah, my dear friend, is there any true riches but this? Selfishness may consume, but love only can possess. Thou hast known more of the ways of life and walked, perchance, in sunnier paths than myself. It is therefore, to me, a privilege to hear how the days are passing with thee and thine, and thus to live in thy remembrance. I do realize with thee that true friendship lives on, fresh and green. The lapse of years, separation, or silence has no power over it. Thou, my beloved friend, hast lived many years, and I appeal to thee to say if thou hast known any really idle hours. It has long felt to me that there is a field for abundance and delightful employment in the heart-vineyard, where the tender plants of affection should spring. I know thy life has been rich in these things, but my spirit is pained at the poverty of our souls, when I remember the inheritance to which we are born.

Though a number of years thy junior, it seems to me I have lived a long life in these hurrying years. Cast by nature in a sensitive mould, both joys and sorrows have been intensified to me. The pulsations of my heart, and not the dial, have marked for me the hours of the day.

Thou hast written an autobiography. Alas! even in thy happy life there must be some unwritten pages, because thou hast no power to write them. I have often thought that no human life was ever yet fully written. There is a depth to the bitterness of sorrow which no language can unfold; but is there not a joy of heart sometimes mingled with the remembrance of suffering, in a deep sense of the Divine love and mercy, that would need an angel's harp to sing its meaning? I think, my friend, that religion is too much set apart by itself, instead of being understood as vivifying our whole nature. We need more simple teaching. I love to hear a friend of mine read the Scriptures, who is a very child in simplicity of heart; in the sweetness of his trust and the innocency of his beaming countenance my soul feels, without effort, the opening of the Seven Seals, the successive stages in which the soul passes in the work of regeneration.

How very beautiful are the lines of Ann Preston for your anniversary meeting! There is a dreamy spell in them which lulled my spirit to repose. How well do they apply to thy own autumn days! Mellow, rich, and ripe is the fruitage.

May the same gracious Hand lead thee on through sunshine and shadow by the still waters of life; and if thou and I should never meet in mutability, may we meet in that happier sphere where sin comes not, nor sorrow.

I seem like thyself to realize that the present are among my happiest days. I contrive to gather some little glimpses of summer at a table under the hanging-basket by the window, and the gold-fish in the vase seem to be my friends. Then I have pictures and books, and a sunny lookout to the south and west. Last autumn I spent a few weeks in a forest home in Central New York for the benefit of my health. I was enchanted by the loveliness of the hills, then in the full flush of autumnal beauty; the foliage was touched with the brightest hues of crimson, scarlet, and orange, blended with the richest evergreens, and I never saw such beautiful sunsets as while there. I enjoy bright colors either in the landscape or the sky, but never knew the same peaceful delight in them as on that occasion.

But I will lay down my pen lest I weary thee, yet ere I do so will say I am anxious to see thy son Edward's anniversary poem, and hope some time to have an opportunity. My kind regards to thy husband.

Affectionately thy friend,
M. RUSHMORE.

The latter part of the Sixth month, 1876, I

received a letter from my brother, giving the pleasant, though somewhat unexpected, information that he intended to spend the following week with us. It was unlooked for at the time, because he had very recently passed a week here, and he seldom made us two visits so near together. But when he came his coming then was explained : the eighteenth of the month was his eighty-second birthday, and he had a wish to spend it with us, believing it would be the last we should pass together. He appeared in usual health, and enjoyed much the opportunity afforded him of mingling with the few of his near kindred who were cotemporaries and yet remain in mutability. While with us he visited both of our neighboring schools and also his parental home, which was his own abode during most of his years of married life. Two days before he left us a carbuncle appeared on his neck, which was painful, and, though not at first considered dangerous, was the cause of his death. He died on the first day of July, 1876, and was buried in Friends' burying-ground at Buckingham.

It is not my design to draw even an outline of his character in this sketch. He had a large circle of intimate and talented friends, who are willing and more able to do justice to his memory. But on my own account I will say he was a most affectionate brother and a constant correspondent; almost weekly I received letters from him, and how much that intercourse will be missed I cannot say.

In a late letter he made a quotation which I fully believe he amply realized in his own life experience:

"It is of little consequence whether acts of humanity and moderation are blazoned by gratitude, by flattery, or by friendship. They are recorded in the heart from whence they spring, and in the hour of adverse vicissitudes, if it should ever come, sweet is the odor of their memory, and precious is the balm of their consolation."

The following letter, which I received shortly after his death, is so appropriate, that no apology is needed for its insertion here:

July 3, 1876.

MY BELOVED MOTHER,—I am unable to express the strong desire I feel to be with thee to-day in thy room, where so recently I parted from thee in cheerful converse with the dear brother whose society and letters have been sources of many of thy enjoyments within the past years.

Neither of us could have foreseen that this pleasant inter-view was never to be renewed in this life, else would the parting have been sadder, and the shock less startling, that brought to us the tidings of his sudden departure to the land wherein life's mysteries are all now unveiled. Often since the visit referred to have I found my mind dwelling upon him; recalling the gentle dignity and genuine courtesy which marked alike his ever agreeable conversation, and the attention he gave to the remarks of others, even when the subjects were so trivial as to be of little interest to his enlarged mind. Frequently I have said to Edward, " I am so glad I have met Uncle William ;" it had been so long since I had seen him, I really did not realize what an agreeable, lovable man he was, and I think he was pleased to have met us, for he gave me such an affection-ate good-by kiss. He impressed me as being a representa-tive man, whom, had he been called more conspicuously into public life and service, would have been recognized as among the most prominent and distinguished men of his time. May his life up yonder be an expanding one, more and more unto its perfect day. I have thought much to-day of how clear every obscure thing will be to us when we enter the border of that life wherein " we shall know even as we are known," and much that seems unimportant to us here we will then recognize the necessity of. Dear uncle, in imagination I look again upon thy placid features, and with the loving friends who surround thee, I take my place, and bid thee another sweet but sad farewell. Is there not something more I can be to thee, dear mother, than I have ever been, to fill the vacuum of this lost companionship? Methinks I hear thee say, the separation will not be long. Ah! are we not glad, as David was, that we can go to our beloved ones whom the Father calls hence, even though they may never come back to us? Truly it was prophetic when he said to thee, "I felt anxious to spend my eighty-second birthday with thee, as it may be the last we will ever spend together." Thee will write when thee feels to do so, and if thee desires me to come, say so, and I will gladly do it. How glad Mary was that her considerate thoughtfulness spared uncle that stageride that would have been so trying to him, in the suffering he was no doubt experiencing to greater extent than he was willing to admit to you. Nor was it his alone to recall her acts of gentle kindness. My love to her and to you all.

Thy affectionate daughter,
MARY C. PAXSON.

Among the many notices that appeared of my dear brother's death, the following from the *Newtown Enterprise* is selected, as containing in a condensed form his leading traits of character:

William H. Johnson died on Saturday last at the residence of his son-in-law, Stephen T. Janney, in Newtown township, aged a little over eighty-two years. He had been for some time afflicted with a bad carbuncle on the back of his neck, which was the cause of his death. He was a man of mark in his day and generation. Possessed of an active intellect, his mind was early stored with knowledge, and through life he was both a scholar and teacher. Pure, truthful, and benevolent, humanity always claimed and received of him a larger share of attention than self. For over fifty years he was a writer for the public press, always on the side of moral reform, justice, and temperance. From early life he bore testimony against the crime of human slavery, and when it was thought a stigma to be called an abolitionist, he was proud of the name. His house was the home of the oppressed, and many a fugitive fleeing from the house of bondage found there food and shelter, and was sped on his northern course. Thus he lived on his paternal acres in Buckingham valley, engaged in the culture of the earth, burning lime, and occasionally teaching school, doing everything he undertook well and conscientiously, but all the while reading and studying, solving mathematical problems, and writing for the county papers his essays on temperance, education, and morality. He was a man of genial manners, so gentle and modest that even those who strongest opposed his views respected and loved him as a man. His religion was that of goodness, love, and mercy, following the teachings and precepts of Christ, but bound by no man's thoughts, ideas, or creeds. Thus he lived honored and respected to a good old age. Some fifteen years ago he lost his wife and sold his farm, and came to reside with his daughter. Here he was at leisure to cultivate his tastes, read his favorite authors, and, as he expressed it, enjoy life. He had a strong constitution, and large and strong frame, and retained his physical and mental energies in a remarkable degree; up to within a short time of his death he walked to Newtown post-office, about two miles, nearly every day, preferring walking to riding. He took a deep interest in schools, particularly public schools, and some twenty years ago served a term as County Superintendent.

This was William H. Johnson as we knew him. Others who knew him earlier, and perhaps better, can give more full particulars of his biography. We only knew him for the past eight years as a pure, kind, genial old man, who would not by word or deed harm or inflict pain on one of God's creatures; who did his best to reform abuses, correct errors, and teach men and women to be true, strong, and virtuous. . . . His memory goes down to the future pure and spotless. His remains sleep with those of his kindred in the shady hill-side at Buckingham Meeting-House, near where he spent most of his long life.

Extract of a letter from Martha Beans, dated Philadelphia, Twelfth month, 1876 :

Thy letter has been received giving the information that you have lately entered the sixtieth year of your married life. How few of the vast number who have assumed those sacred bonds can make that assertion! I have often thought during the present season of your long and happy marriage connection: how lovingly you ascended the hill of Time, surmounting its asperities, and enjoying its green, mossy dells, of which you seemed to find such a variety. Reviewing all the time of my acquaintance with you, which has extended over a good many years, as thee well knows, not one evidence of want of harmony is recorded on the tablet of my memory. This is a good deal to say when we consider how much I have been in your family. I think it likely no one not a near relative, excepting sister Ruth, has been privileged to enjoy the comforts of your home more than I have. And just here I can but again express my sense of indebtedness to you for the happiness this intercourse has afforded me.

The following lines were suggested to my mind by reading a memoir of Philip and Rachel Price, by their son, Eli K. Price, and are inserted here, although out of their chronological order:

Sweet narrative, from memory ne'er shall fade
The impression that those graceful truths have made;
A faithful record of a beauteous life,
Of patriarch, husband, and devoted wife;
With minds to see Heaven's broad paternal plan,
And hearts imbued with love to God and man;
They hand in hand life's chequered journey through
Kept the reward and recompense in view;
No cloud to either dimmed life's setting sun,
Their hearts, their faith, their hopes were ever one.

First from our earthly vision passed away
That patriarch loved, to Heaven's unending day;
Yet shall we mourn, while still is left behind
His prototype, in manner, form, and mind;
The piercing eye, the locks like wintry snow
As his, are clustering round a filial brow.
The wise expounder of his country's laws,
Her senate pleader in a righteous cause,
And little recks he or of praise or blame
Whose conscience has a meed more sure than fame.

May she, the dearest blessing Heaven bestowed,
Long, long be spared to cheer his onward road;
And when they near the mansions of the blest,
Bright visions greet them from that land of rest.

The foregoing lines were the occasion of the following letter:

PHILADELPHIA, 11th month, 4th, 1855.

MY ESTEEMED FRIEND,—Anna has received thy note, with the lines upon the memoir. We thank thee sincerely for them. They are very sweetly and kindly expressed, and of the subjects of the memoir, justly appreciative of their character. Of their son, the expressions are more than just, and uphold an example beyond his expectations of reaching. The concluding lines I fully accede to, as every passing year makes me more and more appreciative "of the dearest blessing Heaven bestowed."

It is very grateful to find the cultivated, intelligent,

and good approve the little work that was the prompt-
ings of filial duty. In having performed it I have derived the greatest satisfaction of any act of my life,—not
from any merit in it or myself, but because it was a duty
that I felt had been neglected, and it appeared an abiding
sense of reproach that the lives of parents so good and
useful should not have been commemorated, and the
memory of them allowed to perish with their children.
On the bed of sickness which succeeded the printing of
the book, the review of life and its deeds presented
nothing so consolatory as that act of duty. I felt that one
thing at least I should leave behind that to some extent
would do good, and help to keep alive that pure and holy
spirit that alone redeems us from earth's selfishness and
errors innumerable. To myself it was the most instructive
and purifying employment of my life. Examples that I
had not fully appreciated while in the ambitious pursuits
of learning and business, appeared in all their excellence
of an unselfish and truthful devotion to the good of their
fellow-beings and to the worship of their Heavenly
Father. I could then see them in their humble lives
more worthy of respect and imitation than those models
who are the ideal of the literary student and the ambitious
of worldly fame.

For thy kind and overjust estimate of the principles
of my public conduct I am grateful. It is truly the
ground I have endeavored to act upon, to serve my fellow-
men according to their true and permanent welfare, as I
think good men will approve hereafter, and as appears to

33

be right in the sight of Him who seeth and judgeth all things rightly. With the guidance of such a principle, it is true I can pay but little regard to the temporary and fluctuating views of party, or to the praise or censure of party men who are short-sighted in their views.

Leaving it for Anna to speak for herself, I am

Thy sincere friend,

ELI K. PRICE.*

* The writer of this letter died on the 15th of November, 1884, in the eighty-eighth year of his age. He was at the time of his death, with a single exception, the oldest member of the Philadelphia Bar. Celebrated as that Bar has always been for its great men, few have excelled Mr. Price in the qualities which make a distinguished lawyer; none has excelled him in integrity, or in the traits of moral and Christian excellence. His loss will be long felt, and his life is a model well worthy the study and imitation of the young men in that honorable profession.—E. M. P.

THE END.